T0286871

REINBOU

REINBOU

A NOVEL

PEDRO CABIYA

TRANSLATED BY JESSICA POWELL

ASTRA HOUSE
NEW YORK

FOR THIAGO AND WARA

Astra House
A Division of Astra Publishing House
astrahouse.com
Printed in the United States of America

Library of Congress Cataloging-in-Publication Data

Names: Cabiya, Pedro, 1971– author. | Powell, Jessica, 1973– translator.
Title: Reinbou : a novel / Pedro Cabiya ; translated by Jessica Powell.
Other titles: Reinbou. English
Description: First edition. | New York : Astra House, 2024. | Summary: "Reinbou explores the consequences of political and societal upheaval, corruption, and violence in modern Dominican society through the eyes of a child in Santo Domingo after the Civil War of 1965"— Provided by publisher.
Identifiers: LCCN 2023035163 (print) | LCCN 2023035164 (ebook) | ISBN 9781662602511 (hardcover) | ISBN 9781662602504 (ebook)
Subjects: LCSH: Dominican Republic—History—Revolution, 1965—Fiction. | Dominican Republic—Social conditions—1961—Fiction. | United States—Foreign relations—Dominican Republic. | LCGFT: Historical fiction. | Novels.
Classification: LCC PQ7442.C33 R4513 2024 (print) | LCC PQ7442.C33 (ebook) | DDC 863/.7—dc23/eng/20230929
LC record available at https://lccn.loc.gov/2023035163
LC ebook record available at https://lccn.loc.gov/2023035164

First edition
10 9 8 7 6 5 4 3 2 1

Designed by Alissa Theodor
The text is set in Warnock Pro.
The titles are set in Leap.

Al fin de la batalla y muerto el combatiente . . .
—CÉSAR VALLEJO, "MASA"

REINBOU

A NOTE FROM THE AUTHOR

Part of this novel's plot concerns the Dominican Civil War of 1965, also known as the April Revolution. The story does not aim for historical accuracy or geographical exactitude. It does obey the interests of narrative and the mandates of the imagination. Its main characters and events are fictitious. Any similarity to reality is purely coincidental.

My story begins with a gringo.

Yes, with a gringo. That's as glamorous as it's going to get.

An ugly word: *gringo*. It sounds like it might leap out at you at any moment . . . maybe because it sounds like *spring*, those metal coils inside a mattress that store up compressed energy when we lie down and release it when we get up, returning, unaltered, to their original shape.

I know I promised you I wouldn't get bogged down in ency-clopedic illustrations or educational digressions. You get enough of that in school. But allow me to break my promise here right off the bat and then I won't break it again, or at least not very often: *gringo* does not, despite all the rumors, come from the phrase "green go," the color in reference to the US soldiers' uniforms, and the verb a pointed exhortation for them to leave whatever place they're occupying. *Gringo* originates from *griego*, the Spanish word for "Greek." It became a pejorative way to indicate a person who speaks mangled Spanish and who doesn't understand a single thing when it is spoken to him, as in: "It's all Greek to me."

And since US soldiers have meddled in almost every single Latin American country at one point or another, *gringo* ended up referring exclusively to the residents of that exemplary country.

But maybe it would be more consistent with the time period in which my story takes place to use the term *Yankee*, originally the name of the inhabitants of the northeastern coast of the United States. *Yankee* is better, yes, because *Yankee* is the word that was used in those days, the word that appeared scrawled on walls, on flags, on banners, and not so much as an exhortation but as an order: *Yankees Go Home!*

The gringo, or griego, or Yankee with whom my story opens is named Julius Horton, captain in the United States Marines.

Pay attention.

Santo Domingo is hotter than Hades and the mosquitos are just dying to tell someone their secrets, especially the marines, who slap at them and sometimes kill them and sometimes don't.

Captain Horton is homesick for his native Michigan, which tells us a lot about just how fed up he is, how bad things are for him, how much he's suffering, because if ever there was a person who hates the place he comes from, it's Horton.

From one day to the next, the years of his youth have become nothing more than a vague memory. Middle age surprised him one day, like an ambush. He served in Korea as a first lieutenant, without distinction. He saw very little action, wrote reports and submitted forms, activities that consume three-quarters of a soldier's life. He achieved the rank of captain without asking for it or deserving it, and he didn't give a flying fig about making major, toward which end he had not, nor would he ever, lift a finger. This was to be his final mission. He would retire, collect his veteran's pension, open a cigar shop, or a corner store, or a mechanic's shop, in New York, or maybe New Jersey. In the meantime, he would have to dignify this ridiculous tropical assignment, taking seriously the "Soviet influence" that had corrupted the constitutionalist guerrillas, and the directive to "save American lives."

If it were up to him, he would shoot every high-ranking military official in the country as unfit for duty (what good is an armed force that ousts an elected president, gets overthrown by combatants in shirtsleeves, and then asks to be invaded by a foreign power?), and then he would drop napalm over the entire rebel-controlled area. Problem solved.

The key to dealing correctly with certain peoples is quite simple: leave no survivors.

The captain can't stand the way the streets smell, or the relentless sun, or the salt spray that rises off the sea, or the miasma that rises off the Ozama River in the afternoons.

He can't stand the local food, or the customs, or the facial vocabulary with which Dominicans communicate without having to say a word.

He can barely contain his disdain for the local soldiers, whom he considers undisciplined, surly, disobedient, cowardly, incompetent in the handling of firearms, and ignorant of combat strategy.

The same cannot be said of the rebels.

In a single week, he returned fourteen of his boys to their families across various states of the union. For purposes of propaganda, the general staff reports a much lower number of casualties, but Horton, who is there on the ground and sees them fall, keeps his own tally.

As always with this kind of operation, Horton tries to distance himself from all the political imbroglios and palace intrigue. He tries and, as always, he fails. Little wars like this one are resolved in offices, in meetings, in cubicles, with phone calls, with press releases, with misinformation transmitted by means of collaborating radio stations, with pamphlets, with defamation and slander, with targeted assassinations. The fighting in the streets, the gunshots, the tanks, that's just the tip of the iceberg.

And to fight that other war, the real war, Uncle Sam requires his intelligence services to be present in the theater of combat.

And there's nothing Horton hates more than having to deal with secret agents.

Especially if they're women.

Major McCollum is a woman, a fact about which no one is in any doubt. Tall, athletic, redheaded, with large, green, almond-shaped eyes, Sarah McCollum is a beauty. Nonetheless, she inspires in Horton that particular brand of terror intertwined with disgust known as "the heebie-jeebies." To make things even worse, unlike Horton, the major is smitten with the country. She finds everything beautiful: the river, the salt spray, the smell, the people, her liaisons in the Dominican army, the spies she directs. But this fascination only accentuates Horton's repugnance for McCollum, since he knows all too well that, despite her enchantment, no matter how beautiful and exotic she finds everything, the major's tactics remain unaffected by any bias whatsoever. Not in the slightest. He has seen her in action during several interrogations.

Nothing like a psychopath in an intelligence post.

And so, when Corporal Jackson brings him the message that he is to report to McCollum, Horton curses his luck and feels homesick for the little town of Ypsilanti, Michigan, which he'd left behind so many years ago, like a dog kicking dirt over a turd, vowing never to return.

Horton steps into McCollum's office smoking a cigar, just for the hell of it, to provoke the major, to force her to tell him to put it out. But McCollum, who is smoking a similar cigar, motions him over.

The major's head is bandaged. The dressing covers her right eye. Horton understands that it would not be prudent to ask about it. He stands at attention and salutes.

McCollum does not return the salute, but extends an arm and holds out an envelope. Horton takes it. Opens it.

Inside, there is a report on movements, hideouts, known associates, family members and habits, accompanied by a black-and-white photo of a tall, Black man of erect bearing, wearing thick glasses and dressed in a chacabana and crisp black pants.

"Alive," says McCollum.

Horton returns everything to the envelope. He salutes McCollum.

He leaves the office.

Later, well, later he would go completely crazy and would never wax his mustache again, or bathe for years, or shave, or cut his fingernails, and he wouldn't comb his hair or brush his teeth and God only knows how he would manage to even wipe his own ass, but on that day, the last day of May 1965, Loco Abril looked like an American movie hero. Like Che Guevara, but darker skinned, a touch shorter, a touch fatter, a touch more serious, but just a touch. Dressed in army fatigues like Fidel Castro's guerrillas, like Fidel Castro himself, and although his uniform wasn't new, it was well cared for, clean, it smelled like detergent.

¡El hombre nuevo!

That day, exactly fifty-one years ago, Loco Abril was known by a regular first name, a regular last name, and held the rank of commander. And you didn't dare forget to stand at attention and salute when you came before him! Oh, Christ . . . Could it be that he's been half-deranged ever since way back then? No one knows.

Up there on the rooftop of a building on Padre Billini Street, this soldier, this machazo, this camaján armed to the teeth, surveys from above with a pair of binoculars, searching, studying, keeping watch. What's that? What's he watching, or whom? Oh, a man as tall as a bamboo shoot dressed in his good pants and good shoes and a starched and ironed short-sleeved chacabana, stiff as the hide on a drum, because Doña Alicia doesn't mess around and she always wets the clothes with yucca water before she irons them. Nearsighted, the man wears a pair of enormous Coke-bottle glasses in black plastic frames, like the ones Malcolm X wears, or Henry Kissinger, like the ones the Professor wears. He's an indio cepillado, since, you know, no one around here is Black, he's got curly hair, gleaming with Halka pomade, he has freckles on his nose. He wears a chintzy little watch that is never slow and is never fast, and isn't that what matters? He walks calmly, his hands clasped behind his back. He makes his way among the market stalls, he greets and is greeted, he is known by all, a smile from everyone and a smile for everyone.

From each according to his ability, to each according to his needs, thinks the sleek revolutionary up there from his vantage point. *Screw Marx and his mother, too.*

Loco Abril, who, at that moment, was neither crazy nor went by the name Abril, lowers the binoculars and raises his eyebrows, surveying his surroundings with the naked eye, at the same time surveying himself, internally, considering the circumstances that have led him to be standing on that rooftop spying on his best friend down below. If only that's all he was.

That man walking cool as a cucumber down Padre Billini Street, that fool, that *civilian*, that intellectual, is his immediate superior in the chain of command. It's Puro Maceta himself.

Does anyone remember Puro Maceta? No one.

How appalling!

Historians—all of them—should hang their heads in shame. Not a single account of the war mentions him. Not that it would be so easy to do. He doesn't appear in any of the newspapers of the time, he's not mentioned in conferences or lectures. There's not a single published photo of him; not standing next to a dignitary, or happily joking around with Caamaño, or deep in conversation with the Professor, or stanching the wound of a fellow combatant, or teaching in some miserable little classroom, or posing awkwardly next to Inmaculada Carmona, the only woman he ever loved . . . Nothing. And even though all these photos exist, it's as though they don't exist. Anyone who might want to see them would have to come and ask us for them.

No one has come to ask us for them.

If there's one thing for sure, it's that the experts don't do their job very well. The experts are experts at discussing and analyzing only those events that can be found by just barely scratching the surface, requiring a minimum of excavation.

And, as we shall soon see, excavation is perhaps the most important concept in this story.

Because a large part of this story is subterranean, by which I mean that the protagonists worked very hard to keep out of the public eye, moving in the shadows, in secrecy. The other parts of the story could also be considered subterranean, not because the protagonists cared one bit about hiding what they were doing from others, but rather because they belonged to a sector of the population whose activities, afflictions, joys, sorrows, problems, suffering, opinions and frustrations didn't matter to anyone. They didn't live in the country—they lived beneath the country.

They are still there.

Come to think of it, the idea of being underground is much more than an allegory with respect to this story. For example: Commander Oviedo, which was the name of the sentry spying on Puro Maceta from up high, triumphant, invulnerable and powerful as a falcon, would come to be known as Loco Abril and would exchange his aerie for a limestone cave beneath the city. He would become, literally, a subterranean creature.

From the heights to the abyss in a single bound.

This is what is commonly referred to as *irony*. Repeat after me: *irony*. Forget the dictionary definition. When you hear or read this word, just think of Loco Abril and that's all you'll need. And even though Loco Abril's fate will not be the only example of irony in my tale, he is the only character obsessed with the idea of burying . . . And this makes him the polar opposite of my star protagonist, who won't enter the scene just yet, and whose mission is just the opposite: to unearth.

This, we might call *symmetry* or *harmony*.

Don't ask me to explain why.

But enough with the disquisitions and digressions and detours. Enough talk about the concept of the subterranean, about irony or harmony or about lazy and inexpert experts. We were talking about Puro.

Let's talk about Puro.

Let's talk, let's talk.

Just listen to the name his mother, Doña Alicia, gave him. Puro.

Some names take control, obliging their bearers to honor them, to justify them. How many pigheaded Pedros do you know? How many soulful Gustavos, how many unbearable Caesars, how many terrible Ivans? My own name, don't I look exactly like it? Don't I behave just like it? Doesn't it describe me to perfection? I think it really does, but if you want, go ask your father, he's known me longer.

We'll talk about his last name some other time.

In the meantime, let's just say that Puro did his name justice. A levelheaded man, selfless, generous, optimistic, innocent, fundamentally incapable of harboring ill intentions . . . or of detecting them.

¡Un buen pendejo!

Blessed are the pendejos who are graced with oratorical skills, for the ears of the people shall be theirs.

But Puro wasn't a pendejo, and he didn't act like one either. Puro was good, pure and simple.

What a strange concept!

That's right, and despite getting knocked around, the disappointments and the betrayals and the beatings, a good person doesn't change. He can't. What does change is the perception of him held by his friends, neighbors and relatives, who now feel impressed and proud and lured in by the warm aura that surrounds him, by the sense of peace that accompanies him wherever he goes, because the heart of a good man is like an ember that warms but does not scorch, blazes but never burns out, like the bush that spoke to Moses on Mount Sinai back when God still deigned to speak to his people. And he goes from chased to embraced; ignored to adored; hounded to harbored, hidden, defended. Even if they kill him, a good man can never be destroyed.

The true pendejo breaks after years of constant abuse; life turns him bitter and rots away all the affection in his soul. The true pendejo gets the pendejo knocked out of him and gradually becomes a cabrón, a son of a bitch, which is precisely the secret goal of the cabrones and sons of bitches, opportunistic expendejos themselves, who subjected him to the harsh education of their abuse.

Every adult cabrón was a huge pendejo as a child. Never forget it.

Puro walks calmly among the vendors and barterers who have set up their stalls along Padre Billini Street.

It's Sunday. The men walking along the streets, both combatants and noncombatants, wear white short-sleeved cotton shirts and khaki pants. The women, combatants and noncombatants, wear lightweight spring skirts and dresses. You can easily tell the combatants from the noncombatants: the combatants are armed to the teeth.

You could argue that even those who aren't armed are combatants, since they all collaborate in one way or another in the titanic task of keeping the US Marines at bay. A combatant is not only a person who shoots guns.

They're surrounded. Trapped inside a scant five square kilometers of narrow streets and colonial buildings. There are marines all around the perimeter, and beyond, floating in a patch of debris deposited by the Ozama River, the USS *Boxer* bobs atop a choppy, neurotic, restless Caribbean Sea.

None of this seems to matter to anyone.

They have run off the coup forces, which retreated in disorder to the San Isidro Air Base where, it was rumored, its generals wept bitter tears. As per usual when any of his favorite little bullies gets walloped, Uncle Sam sent reinforcements to help the weepy generals who had come up with the marvelous idea of overthrowing the country's first democratically elected president after more than thirty years of bloody dictatorship: Professor Juan Bosch.

Let's take a moment of silence, in honor of the brilliant contributions made by the United States toward the development of democracy in the region.

The intervention benefited as well from the support of the Organization of American States, whose member states supplied 1,727 Paraguayan, Honduran, Costa Rican, Brazilian, Salvadoran and Nicaraguan troops, sent off to die for their ideals, led by the very snazzy and very Brazilian General Hugo Panasco Alvim.

That is to say, the same organization that had imposed an embargo on the Dominican Republic as a strategy meant to speed along the fall of the dictatorship was now helping the very same generals who had been created, nurtured and advanced by that dictatorship to wriggle out of the predicament they had gotten themselves into when they ousted one of the dictator's most persistent and formidable enemies.

Another moment of silence, please, in honor of Latin American solidarity and the rule of law.

Far from the hustle and bustle, in a deserted little square on the corner of Padre Billini and Hostos, four boys armed with rifles laugh as they fool around with one of the weapons. The one with the readiest laugh, let's call him Toñito, shows the others how to release the safety.

"Not there," he says. "Here . . ."

They hear the sound of the spring and they all burst out laughing.

All at once they fall silent and stand at attention.

Puro, his hands clasped behind his back, is standing there, considering them. The youths look at him, look at one another, look at him, look at one another again. They are ashamed.

Puro approaches Toñito and takes the rifle delicately away from him. He inspects it.

"What is it you find so funny?" he asks. No one answers. Puro returns the rifle and takes another one. He looks it over.

"Does this all seem like some sort of joke to you?"

Puro gives the rifle back, takes another. The same.

"A bit of theater."

He returns the rifle. An armed combatant is walking toward them, on his way to the nearby marketplace, his right arm in a sling.

"Cucuso," Puro calls to him.

"Commander."

"Do me a favor," says Puro, "for the edification of these boys here."

Cucuso takes his arm from the sling and shows his gape-mouthed audience a bloody stump from which a piece of his humerus protrudes. Puro takes the last of the rifles and inspects it. Cucuso puts his mutilated extremity back in the sling.

"Much appreciated," says Puro.

"Any time," says Cucuso and goes on his way.

"Where are these going?" Puro asks the smiling boys who are no longer smiling.

"To Luisa's house," replies Toñito. Puro returns the last rifle.

"Not one of those rifles has a firing pin," says Puro. He turns toward the street and calls to one of the vendors. "Tomás!"

"Commander."

"Do you have an extra bag?"

"For you, of course," says the vendor, handing him the bag.

"Put those in here," Puro tells the boys, who obey him.

"If the Yankees had seen you here, walking around with those in plain sight, even at a distance, what do you think they would have done? Asked you for an autograph?"

Puro waits for a response, which the boys appear to be desperately seeking among the cigarette butts scattered on the ground.

"No," Puro answers himself. "They would have shot and killed you. And you wouldn't have been able to do a thing except throw the rifles at them and run."

Puro raps his knuckles on Toñito's head, the quartet's apparent leader.

"Your head," he says. "That is the weapon you should always carry loaded. All right now. Get out of here . . ."

The boys take off at a run.

"And give the bag back to Tomás when you're finished!"

Puro continues on his way, walking slowly, and now he's on the last stretch of Padre Billini before coming to Arzobispo Meriño. He approaches a group of people who greet him enthusiastically. They chat. What do they chat about? This and that. That and this.

Puro doesn't know that Oviedo is watching him through binoculars from the rooftop terrace of a nearby building. Puro wasn't there when they handed out that particular kind of instinct.

But that he also didn't notice that a beautiful woman was studying him, scrutinizing him, watching his every movement from a vendor's stall a few feet away, that we won't forgive him.

Oh, no indeed.

Inma looks at Puro with a mixture of total contempt and abject adoration. She's another one who overslept on the day they handed out useful skills. What didn't she get? Oh, the ability to know who she really is and which things matter and which things don't.

"The president of Ciudad Nueva," she says, snorting with disdain.

She sets a white cloth bag on the countertop. Mario, retailer, takes charge: he unties the knot and pulls out about twenty bundles of cigarettes. He counts them.

"Fifteen pesos," he says. Inma widens her eyes, aware that the contrast between the gleaming whites of her eyes and the blackness of her skin makes her look formidable.

"Fifteen pesos?" she protests. "These are *Crema* cigarettes!"

"Go to Puerto Rico and sell them to the Professor."

"You'll sell 'em all in one day to all these little tin soldiers running around here. Give me twenty."

"Fifteen, Inma."

"*Aaaaaghhh!*" grumbles Inma, exasperated, but resigned. Mario puts fifteen pesos on the counter, and Inma snatches them up and counts them.

Puro says goodbye and makes to continue on his walk. Inma, who has not taken her eyes off him, pinches her lower lip and whistles. A little girl of about ten materializes instantly, holding a gray cloth bag.

"Whatcha got?" asks Inma. The girl shows her the inside of the bag.

"No," says Inma. "The other one."

"Clari has it," says the girl. Inma whistles again, but this time she flattens her tongue between her index finger and thumb, producing a different tone that summons another little girl, identical to the first, but carrying a soldier's olive-green rucksack.

"Lemme see," says Inma. The girl holds out the rucksack. Inma opens it, looks through it, closes it, gives it back to the girl.

She points a finger at Puro.

Inma isn't wrong; her joke wasn't unwarranted. Puro does seem like he's on the campaign trail, even though that idea, in those days, and under the prevailing circumstances, still belonged in the realm of fantasy.

And if you don't believe me and you don't believe Inma, consider this:

A young couple with a baby is coming down the sidewalk. They're friends of Puro's: Jacinto and Eneida.

"Puro, how's it going?" says Jacinto, shaking Puro's hand.

"Not as well as it's going for you," says Puro, with a nod at Eneida, who glows at the compliment.

"God bless you," she says.

"And this little guerrilla?" says Puro, reaching for the baby, who placidly allows Puro to take him in his arms.

"Did you double-check the windows at the house?" Puro wants to know.

"Just this morning," says Jacinto.

"They'll fire on us today for sure," warns Puro.

"Be careful, Puro. Keep your eyes peeled," says Eneida, maternally. Puro gives her back the baby.

"Take care of Lieutenant Olivero for me," says Puro, pinching the baby's cheeks. "What are you still missing over there? Do you need anything?"

"Not a thing, Puro," says Jacinto. "We'll send those crooks packing."

"That's the plan."

"Take care."

Tell me! Tell me right now!

Wouldn't you vote for such a candidate?

Puro keeps walking and now comes across a trio of combatants who are manhandling a prisoner.

"What's this? What's this?" scolds Puro. Genaro, one of the abusive combatants, approaches Puro, salutes, and shows him a paper-wrapped bundle.

"Commander," he says, "this traitor is taking coconut sticks to the Americans at the Hotel Embajador."

Puro takes the bag, opens it, looks inside. He takes out a coconut stick, sniffs it. He addresses the prisoner in a grave tone of voice.

"Provisioning the enemy, huh?" he says. "What else are you taking them?"

"What?" says the boy, haughtily. "No. Nothing!"

Puro sucks on the coconut stick. Pleasure transforms his face.

And what is it about sweets that sweeten life so?

"These are Doña Ofelia's, over on Duarte Street," he says. "If that good woman knew that you were selling her sweets to . . ."

Suddenly, the kid is gripped by panic.

"No!" he screams. "Don't tell her! Don't tell her, Puro, no matter how much you want to! Take me to the barracks . . . !"

He drops to his knees.

"Torture me!" he shouts.

Puro, whose teeth can sink through a piece of sugarcane as though it were the soft flesh of a star apple, bites a piece off the stick and chews.

"How much are they giving you for them?"

"A dollar a piece."

His captors curse loudly.

"You son of a bitch," says Genaro in amazement, and he's just about to smash his prisoner in the face with the butt of his rifle when Puro rests a hand on his shoulder with disarming cordiality.

"Genaro," he says, "escort this young Dominican businessman to Doña Ofelia's house. Explain everything to her and make sure that she is well compensated."

"No!" screams the boy.

"I am confiscating these coconut sticks," says Puro with a wink, "for the cause."

The combatants take away the weeping prisoner, who struggles against them, shouting and begging for them to put him up against a wall, blindfold him and shoot him, to garrote him, to electrocute his testicles, to pull his fingernails out with pliers, to sew his eyelids closed, to chop off his tongue, to break all his fingers, to burn the soles of his feet on a hot plate, to hang him upside down by a rope and beat him with a baseball bat.

You see, Dominicans of that era, from the most exalted to the lowliest, from the oldest to the youngest, men and women alike, were all in possession of a doctoral degree in methods of persuasion, conferred upon them after nearly thirty years of study.

Puro moves on, greeting everyone, and, in the lane leading to the cathedral, he is assaulted by a contingent of children.

They latch onto his legs, clamber up onto his back, hug him, tickle him, bite him, kiss him, whack him with karate chops, immobilize him.

"*Eeeeeehhh!*" Puro exclaims. "My special regiment! My elite forces! How are you? What are you up to? Look here . . ."

Puro shows them the paper bundle of coconut sticks.

"Provisions!" he says. "Provisions!"

Delighted, the children hop about, trying to snatch the sweets away from him. There's some shoving. Some hair pulling. A muffled cuss word. Threats.

Doña Alicia, Puro's eccentric mother, was blessed with many fine attributes; a light-skinned *india*, but for real, straight hair down to her waist, prominent cheekbones, almond-shaped eyes, a compact chest, strong, sturdy legs made for walking over any and all terrain, like a Caterpillar tractor or a tank.

And although there were many things that could be said of her, the people in her neighborhood remember her for two things.

The first is the way she would strut proudly around, saying that each one of her children had a different father. "A chick from every rooster," she used to say, and she had twelve chicks, boys and girls both, Puro the youngest of them all. They were scattered all across the island, each with a different last name, but all with a soft spot for Doña Alicia, whom they visited regularly.

The second is the way in which she imposed her will, administered punishments and rewards, and maintained discipline in a home teeming with boys and girls of all ages.

"Peace!" she would say, breaking up a fight between siblings, the strap in her hand.

"Peace! Peace, I said!" she would scream with every blow she dealt to the child who failed to behave properly at the table.

"Peace! Peace!" she would also say when she brought them sweets and they would jostle about, everyone trying to reach them first. "Peace, damn it!"

"Peace! Peace! There's enough for everyone. Fall in . . . ," says Puro, his mother's son, and the children form a line.

Each receives his ration and retreats, like soldiers in a barracks mess hall.

You see what I mean?

Amazing.

At this juncture, before I delve any deeper into the labyrinth of my story, it is imperative that I underscore a distinction of capital importance, without which I very much fear that we will become irremediably lost among the dead ends and alleyways with which I am constructing my narrative. Imagine that I am Ariadne, the one from the story your father told you when you were little girls, and that I am offering you the thread that will allow us to find our way out, back the way we came, so that the Minotaur doesn't eat us.

I am referring, obviously, to the two kinds of coconut sticks that exist in this country of marvels: the churumbele and the canquiña latigosa.

Pay attention.

The churumbele, also called memelo, jicaco or caco, is a ball of grated coconut covered in red caramel, with a little pointed bamboo or wooden stick stuck into it. Patient people suck on them two or three times before biting into them, and, with two bites, it's goodbye churumbele. The impatient pop the entire thing into their mouths and draw out the stick, clean as a whistle. This type of coconut stick, then, has a halflife of one or two bites, does not lend itself to being sucked on, and doesn't keep unrefrigerated for more than three days.

The canquiña latigosa is a braid twelve inches long and half an inch in diameter wrapped in butcher's paper. Formidably hard, but not brittle, rather it is . . . *latigosa*, which is to say, elastic, flexible. Not like a spring, since it does not regain its original shape after being manipulated, folded or stretched. It is not a sweet for the impatient, because the only thing to be done with a canquiña latigosa is to suck it, unless you want to risk leaving your teeth behind in an attempt to do otherwise.

Left in its wrapper, the canquiña latigosa is nonperishable, no matter where you put it.

The kind of coconut sticks that Doña Ofelia made were of this latter variety.

Don't make that face.

Accept what I give you, when I give it to you, and do not let it go. You'll find a use for it later on, when you find yourselves mired in the forest of my story, which is no Sunday picnic.

Gradually, the children wander off to suck their sugary gifts in peace, all but one girl.

Her hair straight and black, her skin the color of the tobacco leaves you use to wrap up cut tobacco, her eyes brown; on her back an olive-green backpack. Puro gazes at her. He crouches down to speak to her eye to eye.

"Hmmm," says Puro. "Clarisa or Melisa?"

The girl furrows her brow, offended.

"Clarisa," says Puro. "That mug is unmistakable."

In answer, Clarisa merely removes the backpack and sets it in front of Puro.

"A hundred pesos," she says.

Puro looks through the backpack. He starts to laugh. He looks at her.

"Make me a deal," he says in a conspiratorial tone.

"No deals, no discounts, no credit," says the girl, coquettish. Puro looks resigned.

"Can I speak to your boss?" asks Puro, sorrowful.

"You heard the girl," says a voice behind him.

How easy it would have been to kill Puro!

This is what he himself thinks as he stands up. She's come up behind him and he didn't even notice. *It's a miracle I'm still alive,* he thinks. He says it and he doesn't know how true it is.

He doesn't need to turn around to know who is speaking to him, but he turns around anyway because looking at Inma is always a diversion, a privilege, a party, a dip into clear water. Her frizzy curls all done up in colorful clips, her thin arms (that's right: your mamagüela was skinny when she was young), her skin matte black, smooth and uniform, without imperfections or scars or pimples or freckles. And now a slight breeze carries to Puro's nose the scent of the Jean Naté with which she puts the finishing touches on her ablutions, mingled with the scent of Cuaba soap from her spotless little dress and just a hint of the witch hazel she uses to close the pores on her nose.

Inma gives him a hard look. She's not in the mood to barter.

"No deals, no discounts, no . . . ," Inma begins, but she breaks under the influence of Puro's eyes. She summons strength, but her body betrays her. She parts her lips. She has lost.

"It's a good price," she says. She hates herself. If she could split herself into two people right then and there, the new Inma would raffle off the original Inma for peanuts.

"Exactly four firing pins," observes Puro with amused suspicion. "What a coincidence . . ."

Inma is on the verge of smiling but she gets control of herself. Her face turns hard again.

"Take it or leave it," she says.

After a moment, during which he's never stopped looking her in the eye, Puro sticks his hands in his pockets and extracts two crumpled five-peso bills.

Inma looks at the money and looks to the heavens in exasperation. She cannot believe what she is about to do.

"Let's do it this way . . . for old times' sake," she says, sarcastic, and takes one of the bills from him.

One.

¡Buena pendeja!

"How kind of you," says Puro.

Up walks Melisa, indistinguishable from her twin, Clarisa, except for the way they furrow their brows when they get angry. Inma and Puro appear incapable of breaking the link they have forged with their eyes; the girls look at Puro, then at Inma, then at Puro, then . . . Inma awakens from her enchantment.

"Let's go, girls," she announces. "Say goodbye to Commander Flat Broke."

Inma leaves with her little sisters.

Puro finds it hard to start walking again.

Oviedo has seen the whole thing through his binoculars. He can't help but feel compassion for Puro. If he ever met a woman as hopelessly in love with him as Inma was with Puro . . .

He bursts out laughing, because, in fact, he had already found such a woman. He killed her just last night.

Shot her, point blank.

She had loved him, yes, she had loved him, or at least she thought she did. But the plan was the plan and, unfortunately, he could not leave her alive.

It didn't matter now.

The only thing that mattered now was the suitcase.

He had set it carelessly against one of the building's ventilation shafts. Oviedo looks at it and sighs. For that suitcase, he had murdered perhaps the only woman—and what a woman!—who had ever loved him in his entire life. For that suitcase, he was about to betray the only friend he had left in the world.

Well-built, battle hardened, with the smooth skin and little mustache of Errol Flynn, Oviedo, at twenty-eight years old, was the only spectator left in the theater of his own life; the director had deserted, the supporting actors are out smoking in the foyer, and Oviedo mutters constantly from his seat in the balcony: *And what does that have to do with anything?* Or: *Why did you do that?* And also: *That doesn't make sense.* (Later, when they catch him, he will formulate these same questions, and in the same order.)

The same could be said of everyone else's lives too? Everyone is improvising and no one has any idea how to get through the second act, or what awaits them in the third?

No.

Almost no one is that lost.

For many, the director is God, or their parents, teachers, political or religious leaders—in short, their immediate superiors. Others direct themselves, or think they do.

The supporting actors are their neighbors, friends and acquaintances; but also their enemies, who play the role of antagonists and seek to hinder the hero's progress along the path he has laid out for himself, or that his director, real or imaginary, has laid out for him.

And, based on the audience's response, they can tell if the story is turning out well or if it's turning out badly; since it's not written beforehand, they can modify the plot halfway through. No one wants an empty theater; we all want a packed house. And so we adapt to the audience's demands; not to all of them, but certainly to a great many. In this way, the third act emerges as the product of a collective effort—everyone has at least some idea of how things will end since they've all put their own two cents, as they say, into the real-life drama they're attending.

It could be said that countries are also colossal theatrical works, dramas en masse. Ours, at that time, had assassinated its director five years prior, a director who didn't care one bit about the audience's opinion—he had rushed the first act, complicated the second act for everyone except himself, didn't appear to believe in the necessity of a third act and, in summation, had transformed the country's drama into an autobiographical epic in which everyone aside from him played a bit part. Those not in agreement with the direction in which the plot was headed were kicked out of the production or forcibly removed from the theater.

The Professor had won the election in a landslide not for the quality of his first act, not for the lack of pitfalls in his second act, and not for the promise of a utopian dénouement in his third. The Professor had won the election in a landslide because he elevated the supporting actors to leading roles—he placed at the very top of the country those who, until then, had been living at the very bottom.

You'll have to forgive me this political outburst, though you do have to admit that it was rather poetic. It won't happen again . . . or at least I don't think it will.

Night is falling.

The rooftop is deserted.

Oviedo emerges from a house on the building's first floor, suitcase in hand.

"Thank you, Doña Ofelia," says the guerrilla to the sixty-something woman who opens the door for him.

"You're welcome," answers Doña Ofelia. "Anything to keep up morale."

"Of course."

"And save some for you-know-who. That's the only thing that he and Puro always agreed on. The rest of the time they were always fighting."

"I know, I know. Take good care of yourself for me."

"Goodbye."

On his way out, Oviedo passes Genaro, whose men are leading a dejected-looking prisoner. Genaro taps at the window. Doña Ofelia opens the grating and sticks her head out.

"Doña," says Genaro, "guess what."

Puro is smoking in an alleyway, leaning against a peeling wall, next to a solid metal door. He is startled by a sound. He flicks away the cigarette and assumes a boxer's stance. Almost instantly, he relaxes and smiles. It's Oviedo.

They exchange a brotherly embrace.

"You haven't started yet?" asks Oviedo.

"I was waiting for you," says Puro.

"How thoughtful."

Puro glances at the suitcase and looks at Oviedo.

Oviedo nods.

"We'd better get started," says Puro.

"We'd better."

They walk together toward the metal door. They rap on the door with a complicated secret knock. The door opens and they go in.

These days, groups of young people gather in that same alleyway, next to that same metal door. But not to hatch plots, not to conspire, not to make decisions. They gather to drink.

And smoke.

And use their cell phones to call other young people and invite them to come hang out, get this party started.

Many of them piss on deserted street corners, or vomit, or take a shit, it all depends on the night. Their piss, or puke, or turds land on surfaces that were once, back in the day, covered in blood.

Other people's blood, many of them dead, some alive, but all of them just as young as the kids who, these days, instant message one another saying: "Bro, get over here, the party's lit!"

Ah, the divine treasure of youth!

Thin, sinuous, highly suspicious and obviously armed, Molina watches a company of marines mobilizing down México Avenue.

He does not like what he sees.

Physically, Molina looks like a lizard. But since a book should not be judged by its cover, there is no reason we should find this alarming.

Still.

Molina leaves San Carlos, moving from rooftop to rooftop. The constitutionalist combatants have created a system of bridges using four-by-fours, wooden concrete forms and old doors, turning the rooftops into a network of gangways. Buildings of above-average height are either skirted around or else equipped with ladders and knotted ropes. The combatants move about quickly above the city, in straight lines, unhindered by the grid of streets down below.

Molina descends in Ciudad Colonial, sliding down a wall into the alleyway where there is a metal door. He approaches the door and presses his ear to it. He can hear Puro clearly. Molina has the ears of a bat.

". . . Finally, I'd like to thank Rosa . . . for having been so kind as to slip us the ammunition that made all the difference last Tuesday. Thank you, Rosa. Did your laundry basket suffer any ill effects?"

Molina surveys the area.

"It was nothing . . . ," Molina hears Rosa say, as he makes certain there's no one on any of the adjacent rooftops.

"And what about the clothes?" says Puro. Molina hears laughter. They laugh at all of Puro's jokes; they don't even say good morning to Molina.

"Forget about it," replies Rosa.

Feeling a bit more confident, Molina knocks and the door opens.

Molina enters a room packed with armed men and women. Everyone turns to look at him.

"You're talking very loudly," says Molina. "Too loudly. Keep it down."

Puro, standing behind a huge table, presides over the meeting. He raises a hand and silently asks Molina to be quiet and to have a seat.

Molina can't believe it. He laughs. *You're a son of a bitch,* he thinks, and he'd have reason to know. He obeys with obvious resentment, taking an empty seat by the door.

Across the room, on the dais of destiny's chosen ones, is Oviedo, seated to Puro's right, and Molina really and truly can't believe this, but he does not allow his expression to betray the least hint of surprise. Oviedo, who must have begun to tremble when he saw Molina come in, also keeps his face as frozen as an icicle.

He's got balls, concedes Molina. *Or else he's trying to kill himself.*

Destiny's chosen ones have a very peculiar way of speaking. They sound like actors in a black-and-white movie, as if they were speaking, not to the men and women gathered there, but rather to the Invisible Historians who diligently record their words for posterity. They enunciate in a forceful, nasal tone, like sports commentators, like characters in a radio drama, like those solemn dignitaries who adopt an air of gravity and magnificence upon finding themselves before a cluster of microphones transmitting their important communiqué to various international news agencies. Let's forgive them then, for what might seem to you—children of another time, people from a future which, at that moment, had yet to be born—grandiloquent affectations, lofty pronouncements, well-rehearsed orations.

That was the style of the time. Anything else would have failed to command anyone's respect. Anything else would have seemed . . . *vulgar*.

"Very well," continues Puro. "Moving on to the final matter before we close our meeting, I would like to congratulate our undercover agents. We played this hand very close to the vest and, yesterday, our caution paid huge dividends. Oviedo . . ."

Oviedo stands. He is quick and to the point.

"Acting," he says, "on intelligence gathered by our infiltrators, yesterday, at twenty-three hundred hours, we intercepted two of the Triumvirate's messengers as they were walking to the marines' headquarters. They were carrying this . . ."

Oviedo places a large wine-colored suitcase on the table . . . and falls silent.

One of the audience members takes the bait.

"What is it?"

Oviedo slaps his hand down violently on the suitcase.

"This . . ." he says. "This is five hundred thousand dollars in gold that the United States government loaned to the Council of State, which the marines are demanding be repaid as a 'war tax.'"

Surprise reverberates through the audience like concentric waves in a clear pond.

"This," Oviedo continues, pleased by the effect his words are having on his audience, "is irrefutable proof that Wessin and his henchmen have availed themselves of corrupt and despicable mercenaries who . . ."

Puro rests his hand gently on Oviedo's shoulder.

Oviedo falls silent.

Then Puro rests his hand gently on the suitcase.

"This," he says, almost tenderly, "is what turns the tide of the battle in our favor."

The assembled, controlling their excitement and keeping silent, shake their fists in celebration. Applauding or exclaiming aloud are not options when in a secret meeting.

"This," Puro continues, "means a reversal with a capital R for the coup forces."

The rebels get to their feet, raise their hands in the air, flapping them. Some do a little dance. Others pump their fists toward the sky, as if working an imaginary lever on a water pump, or a lathe in a workshop, or a press in a sugar mill. Or the breaker switch on a massive electrical panel.

The commotion is only visible. Molina closes his eyes and it's as if nothing at all were happening, as if he were alone in an empty warehouse. But Puro . . . Puro has to work that jaw of his, interfere with that peace, claim the glory for himself with poetry and lies and exaggerations and overblown pronouncements . . . otherwise, Puro would not be Puro.

"With this," he insists, gripping the case, creasing it, "we can buy more and better weapons. Ammunition, food, medical supplies.

With this, they will no longer be able to buy the superior weapon power of the North American mercenaries. Now it is ours to use for a better purpose. We have much to rebuild in our community: a clinic, a sports complex, a school, everything we've dreamed of, inspired by the Professor . . . We even have enough to cover payroll for years for the employees of these long-dreamed-of institutions."

You're so full of shit, thinks Molina, barely containing his nausea in the face of such useless conceit. *Well . . . not useless,* he reflects. Just wait and see how Puro wraps these chumps around his finger with his Sunday speechifying. *You should have been a priest, you cocksucker,* he thinks, and grits his teeth, because hatred obeys its own orders and to truly and properly hate it's necessary to bite, to chew.

Or to curse. Contradict. Pester.

"What good is all that money to us if we can't move it in order to get all of those things you're talking about?"

The first to be surprised is Molina himself. He had spoken without realizing that he was speaking. A bad habit. He really should stop doing that, and as soon as possible. Because that's one thing you can say for that grotesque, oily lizard: he's not afraid to look in the mirror. He examines himself constantly, without mercy, and anything he finds out of place he puts back where it belongs, even if it hurts.

He knows that he's ugly, so he avoids tasks that require beauty. He knows that he's stupid, so he avoids tasks that require intelligence. He knows that he's off-putting, so he avoids tasks that require charisma and social charm. He knows that he's cruel, cold-hearted, shrewd, self-centered and cagey . . . Just imagine, then, the kinds of tasks at which Molina excels.

His outburst was an act of indiscretion, and evidence of poor control over his tongue's will, which, given his particular skill set and personality profile, is an unforgivable incongruence. In the future, he will work hard to be more circumspect and to control his mouth.

And with that, I submit to you that even the most disagreeable people possess at least one trait worthy of admiration.

Take note!

For the moment though, he's already opened his mouth. The damage has been done, and what's done is done. Everyone looks at Molina, the party-pooper, the devil's advocate, the devil himself, the only one still seated, the only one unmoved and unenthused by Puro's words.

Puro, Puro, Puro.

It's all about Puro.

Puro, who responds to the challenge by saying:

"We have managed to prevent the enemy from entering the city . . ."

Molina bursts out laughing.

"No, no, no. They, *they* have succeeded in trapping *us* inside the city. We can't do anything. There could be a million dollars in that suitcase and it wouldn't do us any good. What's in there? Gold? Even worse. It might as well be rocks. We're sitting ducks, Puro. We're surrounded. They know all of our movements. It's just a matter of time before . . ."

"Which brings us to a different topic," interrupts Oviedo. "The topic of the informer."

Unfuckingbelievable, thinks Molina. *Even the circus animals talk over me.*

Among his confidantes, who were a precious few, Molina had shared the opinion that Oviedo looked like a caveman. And he really did, short as he was, with those long arms, that barrel chest and those stumpy little legs . . . Just then he didn't resemble one quite so much. Just then he looked like a regular person, as I've already told you, decked out in his military attire, clean-shaven, hair carefully combed, with his Don Juan mustache. But years later, when he went crazy, that is exactly what he looked like: a caveman. Only Molina had noticed the resemblance. Perhaps he always saw him as he would be in the future.

Another point for Molina.

The congregation's attention was now focused on Oviedo, who felt himself reborn. He would take advantage of the opportunity before Puro snatched the limelight away from him, which he knew would happen sooner than later.

"Molina is right. One of us, sitting here right now, has been informing the enemy of all our plans."

The revolutionaries began to look at one another, perplexed. Molina thought, and he was correct, that the situation was not at all unlike the last supper the Evangelicals spoke about. Puro was Christ, and if Oviedo took just a bit longer to explain matters,

Molina was certain that those present would, one by one, begin to ask their cell leader: "Is it I? Lord, is it I?"

"We were waiting until all members of the commando group could be present," announces Oviedo, looking at his watch. "We're all here now . . . In a matter of minutes, Comandante Elsa will walk through that door with photographic evidence of the betrayal and of the traitor's face."

As though it had been rehearsed, someone knocks at the door.

Molina is closest to the door, but, despite this, he does not get up to open it. He remains imperturbable and indifferent. After a few moments, when the eyes of all those present turn upon him with an unbearable weight, Molina, wrinkling his face in annoyance, stands up and opens the door.

Elsa, a young Black woman, is standing on the threshold, her face an inexpressive mask. And that should have been the tip-off, because nothing about Elsa was inexpressive. She laughed when she had to laugh, laughed when she had to cry, laughed when she had to be serious. She was a single mother, had a harelip, was covered in freckles and, in the opinion of her neighbors, had little reason to be so happy all the time.

Perhaps those neighbors had forgotten that she had two children, a girl and a boy. The girl, the eldest, was national ping-pong champion for three years running. In the Pan American Games of 1963, she beat the pants off the competition and stole the fans' hearts. In the semifinal, she played against Peruvian champion Wendy Sulca, from Apurímac province, who fell face-first onto the table trying to save a ball and broke two teeth.

Her name was Esmeralda, and she beat the Peruvian by six points. Some people take things very seriously, so it's worth considering, when our endeavors coincide with those of others, if it's worth losing your teeth in the attempt.

The boy, the younger of the two, wanted to study industrial psychology. His name was Rubén, but he was killed by a car on the malecón and never even made it through his third year of high school.

Puro had baptized them both.

Molina stands to one side to allow Elsa to enter, but Elsa simply keels over, straight as a felled tree, and smashes face-first to the floor. Dead.

For a second, no one understands what's happening. Puro casts a perplexed look at Molina.

Molina replies with a sly smile.

The smiling serpent, pleased with his vengeance, finishes opening the door, and a North American squadron takes the place by storm.

According to those who were there and who lived to tell the tale, the first to fall dead were three Yankees, done for by the revolutionary Juan Camelo Cortiñas, alias "El Indio." God only knows who they were—all Yankees looked alike to them—but according to El Indio (who they say lived in torment over the triple murder of those three adolescents, later researching them and visiting their graves in Oregon, Alabama and Delaware), the dead were three PFCs named William Connelly, Robert Fields and Lance Smith.

At least that's the story.

The next to die was Rosa, who had been moving ammunition from place to place, hidden inside a laundry basket. Married, three children, the best habichuelas con dulce in all of Santa Bárbara, according to local lore.

And after that, no one knows anything about the order in which people died.

Oviedo grabbed the suitcase, closed it, drew his revolver and started shooting. Puro knocked the table over and the rebels took up positions behind it. Without speaking a word, the constitutionalists opened fire to cover Puro, who was never armed, and Oviedo, who was carrying the marines' gold, allowing them to escape through a back door.

A back door through which, surely, more gringos would be waiting for them, because Molina would not have done a half-assed job of it.

Oviedo and Puro correctly intuit the situation and, instead of heading toward the doomed exit, they climb the building's stairs. The noise of the shootout, so deafening just a few minutes before, fades into the background. Reaching the second floor, Oviedo looks around, kicks open the door to an accounting office, walks over to one of the windows, opens it and jumps, never letting go of the precious suitcase.

Puro drops down alongside him, with much less precision, less grace, clumsy. Outside, the cacophony of gunshots, explosions and shouted orders in both Spanish and English assaults them again.

"That bastard . . ." says Puro, rubbing the knee he had landed on when he hit the pavement.

"Listen to me!" says Oviedo, handing the suitcase over to Puro. "Take the money and get to one of our hideouts. Do you hear me? We need you alive. You're no good to us dead. Come on, get going!"

They take off running through the dark, empty courtyard and come out in a narrow alleyway that runs east to west. They hear gunshots all around them and realize suddenly that they're trapped by enemy fire coming from both ends of the alleyway and there's nothing at all to hide behind. All seems lost, but the rebels have taken to the rooftops and windows of neighboring buildings and they take out the marines who were blocking the eastern exit that leads toward the river. The two friends bolt in that direction.

Unintentionally, but by necessity, Oviedo and Puro run into the packed streets, bringing in their wake the indiscriminate gunfire of both factions, which results in the deaths of innocent passersby. Everyone runs for their lives. The streets empty out in a matter of seconds as the battle escalates. Oviedo and Puro run and run and run and keep running; Oviedo fires his pistol every so often, taking up temporary positions behind cars, curbs, trees, tanks. Puro runs without looking back. When they reach Avenida del Puerto they turn upriver, running without stopping for breath, leaving Ciudad Colonial, San Antón, La Atarazana and Villa Francisca behind, taking cover in the undergrowth along the river's edge. Oviedo takes up a position behind a wall destroyed by artillery fire, patches of its metal gridwork exposed.

Oviedo grabs Puro by the arm.

"Listen," he says. "Go quickly . . . get as far away as you can. I'll distract them."

Puro hesitates.

"Get out of here, goddamnit! Go, go, go, go!"

They run. They run because they are being pursued by enemies bent on capturing them, or killing them . . . killing them, most likely; there's no way to lose them, to trick them, to tire them out. The marines chase them with the same, or perhaps, greater, resolve than that which drives Oviedo and Puro to run away from them. And who is it that guides them, who drives them onward, who points them out when the marines lose sight of them, who warns them that Oviedo has taken up a position and is shooting; who is the unleashed dog who sniffs them out and points in the right direction so his masters can annihilate their prey?

Who else?

Yes. The very same.

Molina.

This is why, when Puro breaks away from Oviedo and plunges into the brush, Molina is the first to take note and to report it. With a gesture of his hand, a group of soldiers breaks off from the battalion and follows Puro, while the rest take up positions to fight Oviedo, who was one hell of a good shot and not one to be trifled with.

During the April Revolution, Oviedo killed Yankees because he enjoyed it. If the Yankees kept tabs—and the Yankees always keep tabs—they surely held him responsible for a high percentage of their casualties.

In other words, there was no marine who wanted to get too close, because they knew who they were up against. And so he bought precious time for Puro, who got away without any trouble.

Oviedo was good, but he was not a magician. He was one man against fifteen, maybe more, and, in the end, the marines close in, they surround him . . . but they do not kill him. Oviedo is reloading when the blow from the butt of a gun to the nape of his neck makes him see stars and he falls, unconscious.

In the fading afternoon light, Puro makes out the rise of an atrocious garbage dump, around the edges of which sits a scattered village, frankly indistinguishable from the garbage.

So many lucky people in the world! Not having far to go to take out the trash translates into cleaner houses and streets free of detritus and waste.

In truth, Puro smelled the place before he saw it some five or six minutes later.

He'd gained ground on his pursuers, but they're still after him, he can hear them, which is why Puro takes a chance and begins to negotiate the slum's alleyways—many of them dead ends—in the growing darkness.

Trapped inside a labyrinth and plunged now into the total darkness of a moonless night, Puro could have gone into any house . . . but he sees a faint light dancing only in a single house and that's where he goes. The slum dwellers, with the feral instincts of survivors of disasters and cataclysms, have interpreted the racket outside with great precision and have hunkered down inside their homes. Even so, Puro could have gone into any one of them. Let's just say that this is not the sort of neighborhood with an abundance of the type of houses that have doors with locks on them.

And yet, Puro heads for the light.

Just like the dead.

He hops over a couple of poorly built fences, comes to the shack inside which shines that feeble light, and he steps inside without further ado.

And inside, sitting at a small wooden table, reading a book by the light of a kerosene lamp, is Inma.

Uh-huh. The very same.

Inma is startled when she sees Puro, and she's just about to scream, but Puro grabs her just in time and covers her mouth. He begs her:

"Please . . . Please . . ."

Inma is terrified, but Puro's gentle manner and his silent pleading manage to calm her, at least for the moment. Puro releases her. Inma looks around and, following her gaze, Puro discovers Melisa and Clarisa sleeping, curled up together on a mattress on the floor. Puro understands her concern.

Outside, the scuffling of the soldiers being guided by the traitor grows more and more distant. A shot, screams, silence . . . Puro and Inma breathe a sigh of relief.

And suddenly there's a thunderous knock at the door.

1976

The bad thing about telling a story to two people is that, as sure as the sun rises, each one will want something different from the story. Telling a story to just one person is a snap; they'll be satisfied with whatever they hear, because the person telling the story will tailor it to the listener's questions and concerns without the story losing its essence. Telling a story to a group of people is easier still, since they either stay quiet or else there's no story.

But two people listening to the same story makes telling it like walking uphill with a sackful of rocks, especially when the listeners are people like the two of you.

One of you wants me to tell about your grandpa and the war, about how your grandma was a tigress and a bandit, and grandpa was an intellectual and a strategist, and about how the tigress bandit helped the intellectual strategist, and you revel in the gunshots and the bombings and the torture and the gringos falling dead like flies and you stick out your tongue and act like you're going to puke whenever the story veers toward smooches and batting eyelashes and lovey-dovey, touchy-feely, hanky-panky . . . And the other one wants me to tell about your father and how he met your mother, and about how your father was even more of a fool than your grandpa, and your mother more of a tigress than your grandma, and that's why they fell in love, and you ask specifically for details of their romance, squeezing your eyes shut and covering your ears every time anyone puts a bullet in someone, or cuts someone's throat, or hangs someone upside down and beats him with a baseball bat . . .

And neither one of you understands that my story is not one thing or the other, because in this tale—both the grandfather's and the father's—love and violence come braided together. At some point in both stories, one of you, out of necessity, will have to settle for making your requisite faces.

As an act of good faith and so that neither of you runs out of the room in despair because the story that the other one wants to hear is going on too long, I'm going to tell this story in turns. Now that you've put me in this mojiganga, you're both going to listen to the story in a single go, each one sitting through what interests you and what doesn't interest you too, because, in the end, you both need to know all of it. It's important. Many things are explained in this story, questions you've asked me from time to time will be answered, situations that have never made sense to you will make sense.

Be patient, now, and pay attention . . .

A thunderous knock.

Inma wakes up. Someone must be banging on the door. But who could it be at this hour of the morning? Maybe it was a dream.

Maybe it was *the* dream.

It's been a while since she's had it. It doesn't matter if she dreamed it or not, because already she can't remember anything about it. The dream has evaporated.

Inma struggles for a moment to wake up completely, to get her bearings. She sits up on the tiny pallet. Next to her, Raúl, in underwear and a T-shirt, dead drunk. Before her, in the tiny space between her bed and the stove, is Maceta, her ten-year-old son, ironing the shirt of his school uniform on a tiny ironing board.

Everything is tiny in a shack, except its inhabitants.

Maceta is short for his age, but sturdy. His skin is a lustrous black, like his mother's, not matte brown like his father's, may he rest in peace.

He wears his Afro trimmed in straight lines, short, compact, like the merengue musicians on television, not in the honeycomb style—oval shaped, big in the back and on the crown of the head, short in the front—like the salsa musicians from Puerto Rico.

Maceta is a patriot.

He's inherited his father's round eyes, but not his myopia: his vision, like Inma's even today, is 20/20.

Which, when you really consider it, is the downfall of idealists and dreamers, who would benefit from seeing themselves surrounded by a reality just a bit more out of focus, a blurry, uncertain reality upon which they could impose their fantasies. To see things in 20/20, with all of their fine-grained, well-defined lines and angles and three-dimensionality, upsets the mechanisms of the imagination . . . in the majority of cases.

For Maceta, as we shall see, it presents no problem whatsoever.

Maceta was born with the umbilical cord wrapped twice around his neck, in a time before ultrasounds existed, or at least not for people like Inma. So Inma pushed and pushed and pushed, and the cord tightened and tightened and tightened around Maceta's throat, until the midwife realized what was happening and freed him of the noose that had been his lifeline for nine months.

There are times when Inma—who is not stupid, not now and not back then, or before either, when she was a little girl—looks at Maceta, so serious, so even-tempered, so stoic, so, as Puro would have said, *peculiar*, with his way of being in this world and, at the same time, in another world altogether, and she wonders if the cause wasn't that brief lack of oxygen to his brain when he was born. She's heard it said, or maybe she read it somewhere: the brain needs oxygen in order to function and to maintain all its parts optimally calibrated. If some parts die or malfunction due to a lack of oxygen, the flaw is noticeable and the person who bears it is incapable of carrying out certain functions normally, such as retaining information, speaking, walking, thinking . . .

But Maceta is perfect. At the top of his class, a voracious reader, an ace at math, studious, diligent, responsible, mature beyond his years, eloquent, persuasive, curious, possessor of an immense and varied vocabulary. An old soul.

And Inma thinks that maybe we all have a part of our brain that sabotages us, that holds us back, that throws sand in the oil, sugar in the gas tank, soap in the sancocho, and prevents us from being the best version of ourselves.

And this was the part that the two loops of umbilical cord strangled out of Maceta's brain.

She thinks it now as she watches Maceta ironing and putting a finger to his lips, pointing to his little sister, the baby just a few months old, asleep in a basket on the floor, daughter of her union with Raúl, the saltapatrás half-drunk and sleeping at her side.

When he finishes ironing his shirt, Maceta puts it on, buttoning it all the way up to his neck, and proceeds to slowly pour the water he'd already boiled on the stove through a long, brownish mesh filter until the coffee pot is full.

Now he needs his shoes, which requires him to step carefully over the bedroll on the floor, upon which sleep his aunts, Clarisa and Melisa, two fully grown women, beautiful, half-naked, because the heat inside a shack is a function of the square root of its occupants. But, since the mosquitos are worse than the heat, Maceta covers his aunts with the threadbare sheet lying in a tangle between them.

Maceta moves to his bed, a padded box attached to the wall like a drawer; he crouches under it and pulls out a pair of shoes, which he proceeds to shine expertly. He has worked, ever since he was very young, as a shoeshine boy. When he finishes, he puts on his socks and then his shoes. Once they're on, he goes to the stove, where there's a glass baby bottle filled with rice milk in a pot of water, standing upright like a soldier, as dictated by the bain-marie protocol. Maceta grabs it, puts a drop on his wrist to test the temperature and then begins to feed the baby.

Inma, never noted for her optimism, had named her Amparo.

Inma finally gets up and carefully takes the baby from Maceta to keep feeding her. The two girls also wake up, stretching their shapely arms and their long legs, fluffing their limp manes of hair. They stand up, caress Maceta's head, kiss him, and serve themselves a cup of coffee. Everyone gets ready to start the day, exchanging endearments . . . except Raúl, who is still asleep. No one says a thing. Maceta puts on his backpack, accepts a cup of coffee and a piece of bread from Clarisa, and leaves the shack.

It's almost spring and getting lighter in the early mornings. Maceta sits on an old, overturned powdered milk tin and eats his breakfast.

He guesses that it will be a sunny day, with few clouds, hot. From the nearby river emanates a miasma of dead fish guts, rotten lilies and diesel. Around him, the familiar landscape: the husk of a burned-out Volkswagen Beetle; buckets of varying colors and sizes (each with a specific function); a badly pruned Maltese cross hedge; concrete blocks in diverse states of physical integrity; the un-whitewashed wall of a house that never was; a power line laden with tennis shoes; the communal water tap, always dripping; stray dogs that sniff in Maceta's direction, coveting his piece of bread, but fearful, because Inma has already taught them a lesson several times, and an enormous, leafy tamarind tree on the edge of the unpaved street, under which, in the afternoons, his aunts do each other's hair before heading off to work.

The neighborhood begins to gradually wake up and the street becomes peopled with men and women heading off to earn their living in various ways. Men push their tricycle carts, women carry water in heavy cans atop their heads, mongrel dogs amble past, motorcycles with three or more passengers buzz by, street vendors show off their wares, coffee vendors serve small cups to their clients . . .

And Maceta, with his piece of bread in one hand and his cup of coffee in the other, feels like the luckiest boy on planet Earth.

When he finishes his breakfast, Maceta stands up. He is impeccable in his school uniform. No. Not impeccable. A small stain on his shoe catches his eye. He wets his finger, bends over and eliminates it. Satisfied, he grabs his backpack and begins to walk.

For Maceta, the best part about living in a neighborhood like his is the intimacy of its spaces. Obviously, at his age, Maceta was not in possession of the analytical apparatus that would have allowed him to express it in that way, but let's read his mind and take a few liberties, okay?

From the front of his shack, it's just two steps to the right and we're at Mercedes's shack, the jamona who works as a seamstress; one step further and you come to the little cement house of Don

Jorge Aníbal, the old cane-field foreman who lives with a group of retired sugarcane cutters from Puerto Plata; three more steps and we're at Abulraziq's, the old Palestinian patriarch who runs an upholstery shop with his many sons.

Ten steps to the back and bordering his own house, past an acerola bush and a tangle of ahuyama vines that appear to have trapped, among their tentacles, the tractor trailer without wheels that's been lying in the same place since before Maceta can remember, and we've arrived at Don Goyo's, the hermit who sells ornamental plants. Five steps to the front and Maceta crosses the street toward Lidio López Gutiérrez's Auto Body and Paint Shop, as the sign hanging above the door proudly announces. The shop is on the corner, and the street peters out in a straight line toward other shacks, almost all of them built of wood and scrap, and houses made of cinder blocks and cement, since there are some of these in the neighborhood too, sometimes even with two stories and a balcony. This is the route Inma takes to work.

To get to school, Maceta takes the route to the left.

His lungs filled with the rarefied air coming off the river, bringing him a sense of peace and tranquility, and comforted by the various and familiar odds and ends that are always scattered about, almost all of them unsalvageable parts from cars Lidio had fixed at some point or another, Maceta sets off for school.

Four steps and he's in front of Don Chago's, whose vegetables and groceries and fruits are beautifully arranged in the basket of his tricycle cart. But Don Chago appears to be having serious problems with the chain and is not ready to make his rounds.

"Good morning, Don Chago," says Maceta.

"Good morning, Maceta," replies Don Chago. "Learn something good today so you can teach it to me."

They both start laughing.

"I'm serious! I'm sick of selling lettuce!"

Three more steps and Maceta comes to a couple standing in front of a shack, using a bucket to pour water on themselves and their five sons of varying ages.

"Good morning, Don Jacinto," says Maceta. "Good morning, Doña Eneida."

"Good morning, mijo!" says Don Jacinto.

"Good morning, Maceta!" says Doña Eneida.

Maceta makes a show of taking a huge lungful of air.

"Good morning, Olivero, Jacintico, Juan Matías, Garibaldi and William Sócrates!" he shouts.

The aforementioned respond in unison:

"Good morning, Maceta!"

Three steps further, only three more steps, Maceta passes by the grocery owned by Don Tomás, who is quarreling with his son, Simón, just outside the door. They always argue about the same thing at the same time of morning, every blessed day.

Simón is sitting astride his motorbike, ready to start it up, but his father will only let him go after having carefully inspected the list of deliveries, already packed in the basket.

"¡Virgen de la Altagracia! Don't argue with me!" despairs Don Tomás. "Go to Doña Aura's house first, then take Duarte and deliver the rest that way . . ."

"Oh, Papá," interrupts Simón, "I can take Duarte first and then go to Doña Aura's after."

"Oh, sure!" cries Don Tomás in triumph. "But if you do it that way you'll be going the wrong way down that little one-way street you like to take as a shortcut. I know you, dummy! I don't want another accident!"

"Good morning, Don Tomás . . ." says Maceta, not slowing his pace. "Good morning, Simón."

"Good morning, mijo," says Don Tomás, tempering himself.

"Good morning, Maceta," says Simón, grateful for the détente.

Father and son watch Maceta walk up the street, away from the grocery, then look at one another again, suddenly remembering their topic of conversation.

"Look, you know what?" Don Tomás relents. "Do whatever you want."

"It's okay," Simón surrenders. "I'll do it your way."

Maceta continues along his way to school, but he stops suddenly and bends over to retrieve something from the ground. Curious, he considers the object in the palm of his hand.

Other people would recognize the object as a simple glass marble, a white ball sticking up from the ground it's been trampled into, a shooter with multicolored horizontal veins.

People with simple minds that house simple ideas about the simple world in which they live.

For Maceta, however, nothing is what it appears.

Appearance is an object's most deceptive trait, a visual, tactile, olfactory and, at times, also a gustatory ruse. A distraction. Maceta sees straight through appearances. His eye is a laser beam, as are the rest of his senses.

Maceta cleans the marble and looks at it in the sunlight. Immediately, he comprehends the nature of the object he holds in his hands. He takes a small notebook from his backpack, turns the pages and begins to write.

> **POCKET JUPITER.** *Sphere with bands of color representing different atmospheric strata. Great Red Spot absent, possibly in formation: observe over the following months in order to detect its gradual appearance. Deceptive solidity, produced, perhaps, by a time-space discrepancy. Fallen from the sky, without a doubt.*

Maceta closes the notebook, stuffed full of similar entries recording other rare and marvelous discoveries, puts it away in his backpack, pockets the marble . . . I mean, the *Pocket Jupiter*, and starts walking again, smiling, oblivious to the people around him who, alert and panicked, are running away in terror.

Mothers grab their children and shut themselves inside their houses. Others run as though fleeing some great danger. Men pick up their pace. The street rapidly becomes deserted.

Maceta doesn't even notice. He's spotted something else on the ground and he bends down. It's a spark plug. Before him, suddenly, a pair of feet appears, covered in filthy, tattered plastic grocery bags. Maceta looks up and sees the formidable figure of a ragged, dirty, savage-looking man, his face hidden behind a prominent beard, and crowned with a very unkempt Afro. Some sort of hirsute creature trying to pass as a man and failing miserably.

How the mighty have fallen.

"With the same yardstick they used to measure me, you will measure them," says the humanoid monster. Maceta stands up, unfazed by the apparition. "Loco Abril," Maceta inquires, guileless, "what's this thing?" As an answer, the savage snatches the spark plug from his hands, looks at it, throws it far away and takes off running. Maceta looks at him in puzzlement, then laughs, searches for the spark plug and puts it in his pocket.

He comes at last to a street where he joins with other students in school uniforms, the great river into which all tributaries converge. A small civilization in light blue and khaki, marching off to the conveyor belt that will deliver them to their respective future miseries.

Wepa . . . This part of the street is in the most "affluent" area of the neighborhood. Here you'll find the most well-stocked grocery stores, the beauty salons with hot water, bakeries and cafeterias under a proper roof and not out on the sidewalk, car washes, outdoor discos, the betting parlors, the nightclubs.

"Molina territory," as Maceta calls it, because so many of the businesses carry that name. Molina Betting Parlor, Molina Consignment, Molina Sports Bar & Casino . . . Maceta had never seen Molina himself, until that day.

At an intersection, a new and enormous sign had been erected that said *Social Christian Reformist Party*, accompanied by a photograph of a man with a big Afro and a painter's brush mustache, and the following slogan: "Molina, Your Congressman."

I don't imagine either one of you is surprised that that reptile ended up in politics.

Blessed are the great sons of bitches, for their survival is assured.

Hundreds of children are playing and talking in front of the school, but let's talk about Lucía.

Lucía Méndez.

In that school, there was not a single girl more beautiful, intelligent, coy, studious, athletic . . . you get the idea. The most popular girl, but not conceited, or vain, or airheaded. What? She got sick and tired of the herds of sweaty boys and the unkempt little minions tying themselves in knots so that she might grace them with her friendship? Well . . . she was a child. We'll forgive her for her childishness.

She's sitting alone on a bench, her dark skin contrasting beautifully with her green eyes. Other kids bug her, pulling her hair as they pass by. She shoots them an irritated look and sticks out her tongue. *They're in love with you*, her mother insists. *Being in love must be the worst*, thinks Lucía.

She's bored. More than bored. She's fed up. *How much longer until the bell? An eternity!* Best not to even think about it.

But then her face lights up.

She fixes her hair.

She starts swinging her legs on the bench, nervous.

Maceta sits down next to her. Without a word, he takes out his notebook, points to that day's entry and, while she reads in a whisper, hands her the marble. She takes it between her index finger and thumb . . . and turns to Maceta with a look of embarrassed pity.

"A planet?" she says and gives him a hard look. Maceta is busy pulling a book out of his backpack, but he correctly intuits the explanation Lucía needs.

"A pocket planet."

Lucía clicks her tongue at him and looks away, but Maceta already has the book open to the pertinent page and shows it to his friend: an image of the solar system. He takes the marble back from Lucía and holds it up next to the picture of Jupiter. Except for the Great Red Spot, marble and planet are identical.

Lucía is amazed.

The bell rings.

They both get up from the bench and begin walking toward the classrooms.

"It's still just a marble," says Lucía, ever the materialist. "You know that, right?"

Ah! School day reminiscences! How lovely they are!

The crumbling blackboards, the dilapidated classrooms, the classes packed with more than thirty students, pupils sitting on overturned buckets or on rocks because they arrived too late to school to claim a desk or else they haven't paid the teacher the seat fee.

Such nostalgia!

Maceta and Lucía pass by the ninth-grade classroom just in time to hear Mr. Eleazar's science lesson:

". . . and then God made the Earth right in the very center of the universe to show his love for mankind . . ."

Mr. Marte's eighth-grade social studies lesson:

". . . so tell your parents if they want you to get good grades they should go this Wednesday to the meeting in support of Molina, the best candidate for congressman that . . ."

Mr. Rodríguez's personal tutelage, as he caresses a seventh grader's hair:

"You want to pass this class, don't you? Well, on Friday you'll have to stay after school for a few extra hours. I'll take you home myself afterwards . . ."

Nothing like a good education!

Maceta and Lucía enter the sixth-grade classroom, presided over by the illustrious and erudite Mr. Reyna, a man of an unmistakably gangster-like bent.

"Lluberes, Leonardo."

"Present!" shouts little Leo.

"Méndez, Lucía Antonieta."

"Present!" says Lucía without hesitation.

"Maceta, Ángel."

Maceta is daydreaming.

"Maceta, Ángel," insists Mr. Reyna without looking up from his roster. Lucía whacks Maceta on the head. Maceta comes back to Earth.

"Present!" he shouts. Everyone in the classroom starts laughing.

A kite without a string is carried off by the wind. A string without a kite becomes tangled, dead on the ground.

There are perfect couples, just so you know.

The years have been tough on Inma and the maid's uniform doesn't help.

There are so many tasks to do in the Horton home. First, Inma mops the floor of the elegant and luxurious living room. Marble. The marble is mopped with plain water; none of those perfumed bleaches. Mrs. Horton has explained it a thousand times. She reminds Inma every single day, as if she's forgotten that she's said it the second it comes out of her mouth, or as if convinced that Inma were unsurpassably stupid, incapable of remembering important things for longer than a few minutes, constrained by the limits of a congenital mental and, who knows, even racial, retardation.

These Dominicans . . .

But Mrs. Horton . . . Mrs. Horton is Dominican, no matter how hard she tries to forget it.

Maybe the issue of national identity is a matter of opinion.

Inma moves the bucket and surveys her work. The floor looks like a mirror . . .

Too bad Capitan Horton's two rottweilers come in just at that moment and muddy the entire thing all over again.

"Brutus! Caesar!" the old gringo calls to them, commanding. And, yes, now we are in a time when we use the word *gringo*.

Gringos get old too, and Horton's gone bald to boot. If Inma had access at that moment to a submachine gun, she'd shoot both dogs and master full of holes. But there's no submachine gun, and that's that. Things are what they are and there's no bullet in the world that can change them. She knows that all too well. Take it, deal with it, shut up. She adheres to these three imperatives in the hope of making it to old age in peace, and from there to the grave, without too many jolts along the way, since asking for happiness and comfort is like trying to shit above your ass, as her father used to say, may he rest in peace.

And speaking of shit and asses, Caesar obeyed Horton, but Brutus didn't, taking the opportunity to squat right in the middle of the living room and leave a little gift for Inma, such an adorable dog. Shit and mud on the smooth mirror of the floor that Inma had polished with nothing but elbow grease, since mopping with plain water is not for anemic little girls, but rather for brawny, meaty, dark-skinned women like her, a boat of average length, broad in the beam, short in the bow and heavy astern, proven against capsizing even in the strongest winds and the highest tides.

Nothing for it. Pick up the turds and mop the floor again. Oh! You think she had another option? Horton left with the dogs and didn't even notice what they'd done, didn't even notice that she was there, industrious, real, three-dimensional, concrete. Was she an invisible woman, a ghost, a machine? Best not to think about it, because then she goes back to fantasizing about the submachine gun and she has too much work to do to lose herself in daydreams.

The day is long and it's just beginning.

Inma mops the floor of the enormous kitchen, scrubs the countertops, cleans the refrigerator, cleans the stove and degreases the oven, puts the beans on to boil, puts the laundry in the washing machine.

Now she turns her attention to the yard. She puts on a pair of rubber gloves, grabs an old tin can and picks up the dog poop that blemishes the lawn of that beautiful garden, while Brutus and Caesar bark furiously at her through the chain-link fence of the dog run.

She throws everything into the garbage bin. She goes into the kitchen, washes her hands. It's time to head up to the second floor.

Inma cleans the toilet in the luxurious bathroom. Scrubs the tub, the sink, the bidet. Mops, hangs clean towels.

Time to turn off the beans. She goes downstairs. Turns off the beans.

Goes upstairs.

Enters the bedroom. Dusts. Makes up the king-size bed with all its bolsters and throw pillows, sweeps and mops the floor, vacuums the curtains, tidies the closet.

Time to cook the rice. She goes downstairs. Puts the rice on, seasons the meat.

Time to take the laundry out of the washing machine and put it in the dryer. Time to gather up the clean clothes and iron them.

Time to sweat.

Time to check the rice, time to cook the meat.

"Inmaculada."

Inma leaves the stove, dries her hands on her apron and stands at attention before a woman who's younger than she is old, whiter than she is Black, thinner than she is fat. Her hair browner than it is blond, her breasts smaller than they are full, her rear end flatter than it is round. Her mouth is thinner than it is thick, her nose hooked, like a parrot's beak, which makes her look as though she's always scowling.

Her eyes are more half-open than they are half-closed. Her forehead large and smooth, her voice monotone and sharp-edged. The combined effect is one of perpetual annoyance, more calm than belligerent. This is not a woman who surprises others or who is herself surprised. She's on top of any and all dangers, real or imagined. She doesn't mince words; she doesn't mean to offend, but if she does offend, she doesn't care. This person is less woman than force of nature, but not a hurricane-force wind, or a tsunami or a tornado, but rather a downed banana tree in the middle of the road, a boulder in the river that stops up the current, a crack in the foundation.

"Yes, ma'am," Inma says with acutely controlled respectfulness.

"I thought I told you not to go in my closet," says Mrs. Horton.

"I have not gone into your closet, ma'am," Inma lies.

"If you have to iron my clothes after they're dry," Mrs. Horton continues, as if Inma hadn't spoken, "do it in the service area. When you've finished, leave them on my bed and I'll hang them up later."

"That's what I did, ma'am."

"I asked you to please not go into my closet. Do not go in there, period."

"No, ma'am."

"When you go in there your smell lingers and you know I can't stand that, I've already told you."

"Ma'am . . ."

"I just went in there and I almost fainted from the stench . . ."

"But . . ."

"I do not want to have to tell you again. The next time I'll just fire you. Is that clear?"

"Yes, ma'am."

The woman turns around and leaves, taking short, careful, little steps, as though she were walking on eggshells, enveloped in a cloud of Shalimar.

Inma redirects her attention to the stove, to the rice, which needs to be stirred, to the meat, which is already starting to sear, and her eyes don't become wet with tears, even though that's what they're for, to lubricate her eyes, which are dry, irritated and stinging.

How the mighty have fallen.

1965

What is the fundamental difference between a person who says, "I'm thirsty" and one who says, "I want water?"

The door of the shack opens with a violent kick and three marines come in like a tempest.

"Where is he?" one of them asks.

"What?" Inma says, playing the fool, and she still hasn't closed her mouth when one of the soldiers closes it for her with a slap. Inma falls to the ground.

Clarisa and Melisa, who had been sleeping on the floor, wake up screaming and cling to each other. The other soldiers start searching the small space, upending everything. The soldier who had smacked Inma stands over her, looking at her naked legs. She tries to cover herself.

"He's not here," one of the marines announces. They look at one another, then at Inma, lying defenseless on the ground, and the one who knocked her down tells the others:

"Guard the door."

Don't make that face. This is what wars are for.

The two marines step out, close the door and take up a post outside to give their companion time. They'll have their turn soon enough. The soldier who stayed inside the hut with Inma begins unbuttoning his pants.

"No . . ." Inma says.

The soldier kneels and grabs Inma by the legs.

"Come on, baby . . ." says the boy, an overgrown kid really, a pup. Inma struggles.

"No! No!" she screams.

Just when the rape is about to happen, the North American hero enters the shack, the blond man from the movies, his golden hair slicked back with Brylcreem . . . In truth, Captain Horton is a rather ugly man, but all that whiteness, all that rosy flesh makes an impression, as if reality had been suddenly pierced by a bolt of Hollywood magic, the original home of whiteness and rosy flesh. The rookie rapist gets clumsily to his feet and stands at attention, awkwardly pulling up his pants. Horton watches him patiently. The soldier salutes him, holding his pants up with his left hand.

"Get the fuck out . . ." Horton orders.

The soldier hurries to obey.

"And tell Molina to get in here."

Horton is left alone with Inma, to whom he offers a hand, helping her to stand.

"You'll have to excuse the boys," Horton says in heavily accented Spanish. "They're a bit . . . restless."

Horton looks around the interior of the shack, disgusted.

"I think they see how you live and they assume that it's bueno, no problemo . . . that it's okay . . . You know: like in the animal kingdom. If you can get 'em . . . then get 'em."

Horton spots the twins and stares at them with great interest.

"Muy bonitas . . ." he says, smiling at Inma. "What a wonderful double play, huh?"

Inma doesn't answer, paralyzed with fear. She's not afraid of what Horton might do to the girls, because he's not going to do a thing to them. What she's afraid of is that she's going to have to kill Horton with her own two hands, that she might have to use her teeth, rip out his windpipe with one solid bite, but she won't do it fast enough and Horton will call for help, the other soldiers will come running and they'll kill her and the girls . . . or worse.

Horton approaches the girls slowly, but he pauses and regains his composure when Molina comes in.

"Molina," says Horton, quelling his incipient erection, "you know I have my challenges making myself understood by your countrymen . . . and countrywomen too, of course . . . Especially the countrywomen. Would you be so kind as to find out what she knows, please? Gracias mucho . . ."

Horton leaves and closes the door behind him.

Molina approaches Inma. He looks around and looks back at her. Now Inma is furious.

"A man came in here," says Molina.

"No one came in here," says Inma.

Molina studies her, trying to read her expression.

"A very dangerous man," he explains. "Puro Maceta."

Inma shakes her head.

"Not here."

"But you know who he is . . ."

Molina looks at the twins huddled together on the floor.

"You in particular," insists Molina, "you're not going to tell me that you don't know who he is."

Inma holds her position. Molina looks at her intently, but Inma does not respond. Molina studies her, tries to read her, but it's like trying to decipher a message in the flight pattern of a flock of herons. Molina tries a different tack.

"You're Inmaculada, Pancho's eldest."

"Yes . . ." replies Inma grudgingly.

"*Pffff* . . ." Molina nods, contemptuous, unctuous. "The bootlegger's daughter. Uh-huh . . ."

Molina walks toward the door.

"The dead bootlegger, I mean to say . . . but that's life," says Molina as he hammers his fist on the precarious walls of the hut. And he laughs. "You were so well-off, weren't you, sweetie? And look at you now. That's what happens when you play for the wrong team."

"And what team would that be, if I may ask?" says Inma, emboldened. Molina doesn't find it necessary to hide his surprise.

"The losing team, of course," he says.

Molina opens the door and barks at her from the threshold:

"Stay on your toes. Keep your wits about you. Maybe there's a lesson for you in your daddy's death."

Molina gives the twins a lecherous look, winks at Inma and walks out. Inma doesn't bat an eye. But, after a few seconds, a tear crosses her face, swift, thick, heavy with minerals and salt, and, as it makes its brief journey across her Black cheek, it catches the lamplight and glimmers brightly, like a fleeting star in the middle of a dark night.

Molina leaves Inma's hut and walks over to Horton, who's smoking a cigar with his men.

"Did you get anything out of her?"

Molina shrugs his shoulders.

"Keep looking around," he says, his eyes fixed on Inma's shack. "I'm going to stay here a while longer, just in case."

Horton drops his cigar and steps on it.

"All right!" says Captain Horton. He motions to his men and they leave.

But Molina knows that Puro is in that house, he smelled him in the air of that small space. He's there, or was very recently. Hatred refines the senses, much more so than love.

Pay attention.

1976

The bell rings.

Even though it's the same bell, the dismissal bell has a different melody, sweeter and more cheerful, just try to tell me it doesn't.

The children emerge en masse from the classrooms, running, jumping, roughhousing with each other. Lucía and Maceta talk as they walk toward to street. Well . . . Lucía talks. Maceta was always a boy of few words.

"Anyway, Sandra's jealous because she doesn't understand the lyrics and . . . Also, she doesn't have an ear for music. Me, I just hear it once and that's that. I know it."

"Uh-huh . . ." says Maceta, impatient, looking for a way to part company with Lucía. Lucía appears to be trying to work up the courage to say something until, finally, she makes up her mind:

"Well, anyway . . . math, math. What am I going to do about math? I just . . . Oh, I don't know! . . . It's hard for me. And the exam is in a few days . . . so . . . would you help me study? You could come to my house and . . ."

"Okay."

"Really?"

"Yes, of course . . . why not?" says Maceta, understanding that it's better to say something before walking off than to say nothing.

"Yes!" Lucía exclaims, then immediately gets control of herself. "I mean: thank you. I'll make some little sandwiches and some guava juice and . . ."

"I have to go. See you tomorrow."

"What?" says Lucía, watching Maceta walk off at top speed. "Maceta!"

"Math is easy. I'll see you tomorrow . . . Bye!"

Lucía stands there alone, grumbling.

"But where are you going?" she says out loud, and then, to herself: "Oh, men!"

Men! Men! Be careful with men. Be careful, be very careful!

Men are strange creatures, starting from when they're little boys. They don't live in this world. It seems like they do, but they don't. Some more so, some less so, but they're all always somewhere else.

They live the majority of their lives inside their own heads, plotting, planning, studying routes, possibilities, setbacks. If you ask them a question, they don't answer it, or they half answer it, they drop little crumbs to slake your hunger, to entertain you for a bit, they keep you always on the edge of starvation, giving you just enough so that you don't die.

And if they want to screw everything up for themselves there's no way to avoid it. They don't listen to reason.

And if you love them, you're screwed right along with them. You can't save them, but you won't want to save yourselves either.

Be careful with men! Be very careful!

Maceta takes a different route on the way home to his miserable little shack. We see him running in the opposite direction from which he came, crossing alleyways, jumping over walls and sliding down a ravine until he comes to a narrow paved path bordering a long chain-link fence.

Parkour, they call it these days, or so they tell me.

Maceta walks along the path until he comes to a place where the trunk of a fallen tree blocks his way. He drops his backpack on the ground and sits on the trunk, expectant. A routine. The usual.

The chain-link fence protects a beautiful, very well-maintained golf course. Maceta sits comfortably on the trunk, as if waiting for a show to begin.

The show Maceta is awaiting is not that of golfers absorbed in the complexities of their sport. A golf cart with two of them inside has just parked nearby and Maceta grows impatient.

"What, what? Don't . . ."

The men climb out of the cart, look for a ball. They find it; chat casually.

"Come on, whack your little ball and go after it," murmurs Maceta, who still doesn't exactly understand the objective of the game.

One of the men gets ready to swing . . . but he always stops just before hitting the ball and measures all over again.

"But what are you doing?" thinks Maceta, or says under his breath; he no longer notices these distinctions. "Make a decision. Clobber the ball with that club . . . Wait: clobber, club. They're almost the same word. What's behind this coincidence? Does one have something to do with the other? But, how? Maybe if we go back to the origins of both words we would find a common factor . . . Or maybe we would find that the words are completely different and that it's only time that has made them grow similar. These are things I'll never know . . ."

Maceta breathes a sigh of exasperation. The man hits the golf ball at last.

"Finally!"

Maceta applauds happily. The men climb back into the golf cart and drive away. The green is completely empty.

The sun shines radiantly. On Maceta's face, an expression of pure anticipation.

"Maybe it's some sort of automatic mechanism," Maceta thinks or says. "A clock that, at just the right time, sends a signal to another mechanism that triggers the switch. How this is achieved, how a mechanism can send a signal to another mechanism so that it behaves in this way or in that way . . . Well, I can imagine it, but I couldn't say if what I imagine and the reality of it correspond. Probably not. If it's an automatic mechanism, it's getting behind schedule today. Isn't it time for what always happens to happen?"

Indeed: obediently, inexorably, the sprinklers come on and in just a few seconds there appears a fabulous, pristine, clearly defined rainbow.

"Yes . . ."

Maceta's face is the epitome of delight, pure and perfect.

"There you are."

That white light divides into seven colors is a miracle that has always amazed Maceta. The reverse even more so: to think that rays of light in each of the seven primary colors will combine to form a single ray of white light . . .

Who could wrap their head around it!

But, then again, what other color could they possibly make?

After a time, the sprinklers shut off and the rainbow disappears. Maceta sets off on the return journey back to his humble home.

He passes Tomás and Simón.

"I'm telling you . . . it's an electrical problem, leave it to me," says Don Tomás.

"Pop, I heard it when it died," explains Simón. "I was the one riding it. I'm telling you it was the carburetor!"

"Good afternoon, Don Tomás. Hi, Simón."

"Good afternoon, Maceta," father and son reply in unison. Maceta keeps walking.

"Fine, you fix it then," says Don Tomás.

"No, maybe it is electrical. You'd better take a look at it . . ." says Simón.

Maceta passes Jacinto and Eneida and their five sons, lazing about in the bare dirt yard.

"Good afternoon, Don Jacinto," says Maceta. "Good afternoon, Doña Eneida."

"Good afternoon, Maceta," replies Jacinto.

"Did you have a good day at school?" Eneida wants to know.

"Yes, thank you," Maceta answers without stopping.

Maceta passes by Don Chago, who's just getting off his tricycle cart, his basket empty.

"Good afternoon, Don Chago," says Maceta. "How was business today?"

"Good afternoon, Maceta," replies Don Chago. "I can't complain. Did you learn anything new today?"

Maceta thinks about this.

"The order of the factors does not alter the product."

Chago bursts out laughing.

"And what am I supposed to do with that, mijo?"

Outside Inma's shack, under the tamarind tree, Melisa is doing Clarisa's makeup while Yubelkis, a coworker, watches.

"That's how I want you to do my eyes," Yubelkis tells them.

"Clari does it better," Melisa admits.

"You'll have to wait your turn," Clarisa puts in. "Carola got here first."

"But Carola's in the dryer!"

And it's true. The twins have a stationary hair dryer plugged directly into the electrical pole. The very young Carola is sitting under the dryer and she makes a gesture with her hand that means: "I don't give a fuck about turns." When Melisa sees Maceta, she pauses at her task.

"Hi, Maceta!" she exclaims affectionately. "Tell me about school."

"Come here, sweetie," says Clarisa. "Give me a kiss."

Maceta obeys and gives each one of them a kiss.

"Are you going out again tonight?" asks Maceta.

The twins look at one another.

"You know how it is," Clarisa tells him.

"We have to work," adds Melisa.

"Every night," elaborates Clarisa.

"Uh-huh," says Yubelkis knowingly.

Clarisa gives him a nudge. Maceta doesn't get it . . . but he gets it.

"And look who else is here!" exclaims Melisa with relief.

Rounding the corner in front of Lidio López Gutiérrez's Auto Body and Paint Shop, Inma comes down the street, walking toward home.

Maceta runs to greet her and she allows herself to be greeted. As she hugs him, Inma questions her sisters, wrinkling her nose.

"Inside . . . sleeping," says Clarisa.

Inma looks heavenward and briefly closes her eyes, the universal expression of one wishing that the good Lord would just strike them dead, but when she pulls away from Maceta she gives him a true smile.

As if he knew that they had been talking about him, a shirtless man appears in the doorway of the shack, yawns loudly and looks at Maceta with obvious contempt.

"Go do your homework with Melisa," Inma orders Maceta, sitting him down on his aunt's lap. "Clari, go find the girl down at Mercedes's and pay her something."

Clarisa obeys. Inma goes inside the shack, avoiding the man, who follows her inside.

The man looks like a deadbeat, top to bottom. He's just woken up and it shows.

"Maceta has his school uniform on," observes this most perceptive of individuals.

"Of course he does, he put it on early this morning," responds Inma, impassive.

"And may I know why?"

"Because you can't go to school naked. They have other rules, but that's the main one."

"Oh my God, you're soooo funny . . . Now listen here, you little bitch, don't you play the smart-ass with me! I already told you that no one's wasting time around here. Anyone living under this roof has to work, or beg, or steal, or hustle it with the tourists."

"Oh yeah, and tell me something, which of those four options do you do?"

"Don't talk to me like that, goddamnit! Which of the four do I do? I've been out there since last night, working my ass off."

"Raúl, I think that, once again, you're confusing dreams with reality. Look what time you woke up."

"I got in super late. I was totally beat."

"Tell me again: Doing what exactly? If I might ask . . ."

"Doing what exactly? Doing what exactly? Making money . . . doing *that* exactly!"

"Oh yeah? Is that right?"

"Yeah, that's right."

"Hallelujah! So glad to hear it, since, if you've got cash, that means you won't be stealing it from me every time I turn my back, which is what you always do. But I doubt you have a single cent. You're not getting drunk on credit every single day, I'm sure of that . . . Or do you maybe think I'm an idiot?"

"I don't *maybe* think you're an idiot, no . . . I *know* you're an idiot. You're worse than your son. I'd like to know what the hell you're thinking. What? Do you really think that little turd is going to be a doctor, or a lawyer . . . Hum? An engineer? ¡Pendeja!"

"I'm not sure what Maceta's going to be. But I know what he's not going to be: a druggie, like half the little shits around here. Not a day goes by that they're not high on glue or God only knows what else . . ."

"Little Miss Anti-Everything. You don't know what you're talking about. Listen up: not one more cent for that school bullshit . . . Not for books, or pencils, or anything . . . Do you hear me?"

"Ooooh . . . ! Ooooh! Excuse me! Are you really threatening to not give me money for my son's school? Wait, wait, wait: When in hell have you ever given me a cent for anything? Please tell me, since when do good-for-nothing, lazy pieces of shit who never earned a cent in their entire lives tell those of us who actually do make money what we can do with it?"

Since the world began, Inma. Since the world began.

A heavy thud and a scream. Raúl shoots out of the house, foaming at the mouth. Maceta keeps his distance from everything that's happening; he's been lost in thought, looking straight ahead, across the street.

"Aunt Clarisa," says Maceta, "what does it mean to be poor?"

"Being poor," replies Clarisa after thinking for a few seconds, "means never having what you need when you need it."

"Hmm," says Maceta, not taking his eyes off his objective.

"Although," says Clarisa, hugging him tighter, "you could also say that being poor means never being able to have what you want."

"So," says Maceta, scrunching up his face in confusion, "what a person wants is not the same as what they need?"

Clarisa laughs.

"No," she says. "Not always."

"Which is more important?" Maceta insists. "What a person wants, or what they need?"

"It depends."

"On what?"

"Oh, Maceta!"

"On what?" repeats Maceta, not blinking.

"Let's see." Clarisa hates being made to think. "How can I explain it to you? It's almost always necessary to first have what you need in order to then get what you want. It could happen the other way around, but that's very rare. If you can never get what you need, then you'll never have what you want. That's the tragedy of being poor."

Maceta lets it drop and his silence tells Clarisa that he's satisfied.

And from his aunt's lap, Maceta continues to rest his eyes on Loco Abril, who is standing in front of Lidio's shop and staring back at him with equal intensity.

Maceta puts his hand in his pocket, pulls out the spark plug that he found in the morning and holds it vertically between thumb and index finger, holding out his arm as if offering it, or displaying it, to the deranged derelict.

In response, the crazy man opens his mouth and shows him his rotten teeth.

Counting those who are there because they want to be, those who are there because they're being paid to be, and those who are there because they've been threatened, there are two hundred people, give or take.

Rum and beer flow like rushing rivers, and the hoi polloi are out in force. Music splits the audience's eardrums and, if it didn't, they'd be asking the sound techs to turn it up.

Several congressmen, various community leaders and assorted local businessmen have already spoken. The musical interlude—which, aside from raising people's spirits, also affords them the opportunity to lubricate their throats with alcohol without having to pretend to be paying attention to the crap the neighborhood patricians are spouting, a real buzzkill—comes suddenly to an end. It's time for the top dog who's organized the event, the big cheese to whom all the bootlickers previously occupying the podium have dedicated their panegyrics, to say what he wants to say, what he came here to say, what they are all obliged to hear.

Every time he has to speak in public, *to* the public, Molina thinks of Puro.

How easily all those words flowed out of him, jokes, sayings, turns of phrase that revealed not academic, intellectual or pedantic knowledge, but rather a timeless wisdom. This is why his speeches were always so successful. Molina wants to talk like Puro, he wants the audience in his pocket, and it doesn't even cross his mind that it doesn't matter, that the people who are there, waiting for him to speak, will vote for him no matter what he says, because they have other interests that have been addressed, other benefits that will accrue, already promised or granted; they are not there for him to move their spirits, to be led toward a common cause, to be convinced that they need to work together because he can't do it alone and that, in fact, they will need to work hard and make sacrifices.

Blather.

But Molina can't help it. For him, to speak in public means to speak like Puro spoke.

The problem is there's never been anyone like Puro, not before and not since.

And the bigger problem is that Molina tries anyway.

"Friends, brothers, kinsmen and compatriots, children of Quisqueya the Beautiful, discovered by Columbus so many centuries ago. What can I tell you? You all know me, I walk down these streets and you know my name and my address. This is my neighborhood. I was born and raised here. I hustled to make money, just like you all do, and I rose to the top through hard work. I've created jobs by the jillions, I provide work for men and women, no one complains about me and no one's complaining. I've lifted this neighborhood by lifting it from the bottom up!"

The audience whoops and applauds. Molina waits for the excitement to die down. A smug confidence overtakes him. He's already on fire and he's just getting warmed up.

"I have sacrificed much for my country, because sacrifice is a necessary and patriotic duty. I'm not like other politicians who are only looking out for themselves. I'm looking out for myself, and also for you!"

The din reaches a new level of frenzy. Molina feels that, little by little, he is channeling Puro. It's time to bring out the big guns.

"And I am prepared to do what very few ever do. I am prepared to go for broke. If the moment arrives, and it's what is required, I will not hesitate to do as Plato did; Plato, who, to save his people from calamity, in the most unexpected moment, grabbed the hemlock and plunged it into his own chest!"

Hurrahs, vivas, hallelujahs, hosannas. The applause is deafening. Molina quiets the crowd, holding out his hands, palms down, like a prophet on the verge of unleashing a torrent of healing upon his followers. No one can stop Molina now.

"Our neighborhood needs a congressman like me in the lower house, yes sir, so that our voices will be heard in the palace. Because we may be poor, but we're not fools, and it's the squeaky wheel that gets the grease. And don't think I'll forget all about you if I'm elected, like some other deadbeats have done. No, ladies and gentlemen. When I'm congressman you won't see me going around trying to look like someone I'm not. When I'm congressman, friends and compatriots, the doors of my office will remain hermetically open to you all!"

The uproar from the throng reaches its boiling point, and Molina recognizes the moment to take his leave. You should always end on a high note.

He acknowledges the cheers and applause, waving here and there, and little by little he moves away from the podium. But then he stops, as if he's just remembered something, and he goes back. He takes the microphone.

"Allow me to take this opportunity, before I go, to dispel some nasty rumors that have come to my attention."

The crowd falls into a sepulchral silence, in thrall to this invitation to intimacy.

"I've heard it said out there that I'm some sort of faggot . . ."

The crowd murmurs amongst itself, indignant, delighted, held in suspense.

"When everyone here knows that I have a woman on every corner of this entire neighborhood!"

Apotheosis.

Molina drops the mic and strides purposefully away.

Of all the people I've mentioned, Molina is the best preserved. Ugly people have that advantage. Time takes pity on them, detours around them, doesn't touch them. They don't get any better looking, but they don't get any worse. He's let his Afro grow out. He adorns his neck with chains, his wrists with bracelets and bangles. His sideburns are threaded with gray.

Do you remember the movie we saw a few days ago, *Saturday Night Fever*? Molina dresses like the main character: colorful shirts with big collars and pants with wide cuffs. Molina's personal touch to this imported getup is the shiny belt buckle sporting a huge tiger's head.

His office is horrible. Take it from me.

The walls covered in photos of local celebrities are horrible, the furniture with embossed flourishes is horrible, the fake Persian rug is horrible, the badly painted ceramic and crudely carved wooden bric-a-brac that adorns his desk (a dragon, a tiger, a crying clown, a woman lifting her skirt and showing off her backside, a cornucopia, a wooden African standing inside a barrel, with an erect penis attached by a spring that pops up when you lift the barrel) is horrible, the desk chair is horrible, the desk is horrible.

The entire place is a monument to bad taste. The taste of those who want to look sophisticated when they're not, who make ugly what they think they are making beautiful, and whose idea of decor is a deluge of trinkets.

Molina is sitting in his horrible chair, at his horrible desk and next to him is Mingo, who looks like a thug, dressed in a tank top, with a gold chain around his neck and an unkempt Afro.

Mingo looks like a thug because he is a thug. In this case, looks are not deceiving.

In fact, in the strict opinion of yours truly, looks are rarely deceiving. There are always exceptions, of course, but as a general rule, what you see is what you get.

And what you get, there in front of Molina, is a man-child of almost thirty who looks for all the world like a total nitwit.

And, in fact, he is a nitwit. A nitwit who answers to the name Evelio.

Yes. The very same Evelio.

I told you before: *Many things are explained in this story; questions you've asked me from time to time will be answered; situations that have never made sense to you will make sense.*

Pay attention.

Evelio is such a nitwit that he thinks he can soften Molina up by making a pouty face.

"This little business is all I've got . . . It's all I've got," he says. "Inherited from my pop, who inherited it from my grandpa . . ."

Evelio starts sobbing.

"Easy, easy, easy . . ." says Molina, holding the palm of his hand up to Evelio. "Don't do that. Please . . . That's not necessary."

"He doesn't like that," Mingo stresses. "Stop crying. Jesus Christ, act like a man."

Evelio, clearly frightened, contains himself.

"My entire family . . ." Evelio continues. "My entire family depends on my business . . . It's our bread and butter."

"Your bread and butter . . . of course," nods Molina.

"So if you could loan me that little bit of dough . . . to get the bank off my back . . ."

"But of course, Evelio," says Molina, reassuring. "That money has always been here for you . . . The only thing we need is to define the collateral. It's all up to you. What's your decision? That's the only thing standing between you and the money you need."

"Whaddya know, daddy-o? Ball's in your court," explains Mingo.

"Well . . . I would be willing to give you fifty percent of the business . . ."

Molina shakes his head slowly. Mingo smiles sarcastically.

"My friend . . ." Mingo puts forth, "you know perfectly well that's not it."

"You know perfectly well what I want," says Molina, impassive.

Evelio is on the verge of tears again.

"Mother of God," Molina says, exasperated. "Go cry outside, would you please . . . and don't come back unless . . ."

"Unless . . ." says Mingo, mysterious. "You know, boss . . ."

Brokenhearted, Evelio stands up and leaves. At the same moment, a voluptuous receptionist comes in.

"Mr. Molina, Mr. Moon is here to see you."

"Send him in. Mingo, get out of here before that Chinaman sees you and has a heart attack."

"Yes, boss . . ." says Mingo, and heads for the office door.

"Not that way, you idiot," warns Molina.

"Pffft . . . right," says Mingo, laughing. "How stupid of me."

Mingo turns around and opens a secret door, well camouflaged in the wall behind the desk.

"Have everything ready down there," Molina tells him. "I'll be down there with the guy in a jiffy."

"Of course, boss."

Mr. Moon is not Chinese, but Korean, but he's learned that, in this country, it's impossible to explain the difference.

He's short and chubby and shy. Molina stands to greet him and vigorously shakes his hand.

"What a pleasure to see you again, Mr. Moon."

"How are you?"

"Couldn't be better," replies Molina. "Especially if you've brought me some good news. Please, have a seat."

They both sit.

"Mr. Molina, as you know, I'm just a representative. My associates still need to be convinced that investing in your candidacy will translate into . . . better returns for our businesses."

"I understand completely, Mr. Moon. I also understand that if you are convinced, truly convinced, you will do everything in your power to convince your associates and colleagues."

Mr. Moon nods. Molina rises, comes around the desk, and approaches him.

"And so . . . as I see it," says Molina in a conspiratorial tone, taking Mr. Moon by the arm and guiding him toward the secret door, "all I need to do is convince you."

Molina opens the door and he and Mr. Moon walk down a dark hallway, dimly lit by small red lights. Molina puts his arm around Mr. Moon's shoulders and holds him close.

"Do you like our country, Mr. Moon?"

"Yes, I like it very much."

"And what do you like most about our country? Be honest."

"Well . . . I like the weather. It's pleasant all year round."

Moon and Molina come to a glass door.

"The food is good too . . . sometimes."

"The weather and the food," repeats Molina, disappointed, as he opens the door. "Let's see if we can remedy that right away . . ."

Molina and Mr. Moon enter a large, opulent, palatial room, filled with beautiful, half-naked young women. The girls are everywhere, lounging on divans, frolicking in bathtubs, dancing on poles . . . Moon is speechless. His eyes are popping out of his head. Molina takes him by the arm and shows him around the place, guiding him. The girls flirt with him. He's like a kid in a candy store.

"We're not usually in operation at this time of day," Molina whispers in Mr. Moon's ear. "In fact, we're closed!"

Mr. Moon lets himself be led around, offering zero resistance.

"It's all yours, Mr. Moon."

Moon is enraptured.

"Now you can tell your associates, with a more informed understanding, just how confident you are in the investment, and that this humble servant, your best friend in the whole world, is a winning bet."

A girl grabs Moon by the hand and starts to lead him away. Molina stops him and takes him to the other side of the room. Moon looks torn, confused, crestfallen.

"Mr. Moon . . . trust your friend," Molina consoles him, indicating the girls tempting him. "These girls . . . these girls are just decoration. Some eye candy while you drink whisky and play poker and hang out with your friends . . ."

They walk until they come to a red door.

"For men of your caliber, we have a different menu . . ."

Molina opens the door to reveal a red-and-pink room, filled with velvet pillows and transparent, undulating curtains. In the center of the room there is a heart-shaped bed.

Molina gives the awestruck Moon a gentle push and closes the door behind him.

On the bed, Clarisa and Melisa, in panties, smile at the Korean with mischievous languor.

Yes. The very same.

Get over it.

A black van stops in front of Maceta's school.

No, an assault team does not jump out of the vehicle. Nor is the vehicle manned by pedophiles armed with candy and ice cream.

From the van, black as a crow's wing, descend half a dozen nuns in habits as white as sea-foam. In tight single file—they're Christ's army, after all—and carrying heavy boxes, they step onto the campus.

First world countries are their own biggest fans, surely we can all agree on that. They don't hesitate to applaud their own efforts, promote their findings, broadcast their "discoveries," praise their athletes and extol their decent men and women.

They don't waste a single second before jumping into competition with other countries, developed or not, for first place in a variety of areas: imports, exports, education level, life expectancy, infant mortality, minimum wage, literacy, and so on. And yet, there's one area in which each and every one of them are tied and none has an advantage over another. Every single first world country is in first place in believing that they are in first place.

The citizens of these countries don't even realize that they spend every day consuming panegyrics and propaganda. They call these products "the press," "film," "television," "literature," "religion . . ."

The members of these societies cite a long list of qualities that explain their fantastic good fortune. "Work ethic," say some, "racial superiority," say others, "divine providence," "the rule of law," "love of order and justice," "equality," "secularism," they all say . . . Complicated notions that the rest of us cannot understand and to which we cannot aspire.

None of them spend much time ruminating over the strange coincidence that the most fortunate countries are precisely those that invade and bomb and occupy and manage and subjugate and bully and extract natural and human resources from the rest of the countries, the ones that don't invade or bomb or occupy or manage or subjugate or bully or extract natural and human resources from anyone else. In this way, no one can conclude, even preliminarily, that the good luck they so enjoy depends upon the bad luck of others.

And that the bad luck of others, inversely proportional to their own happiness, is a foundation that they themselves built.

What the citizens of these countries believe with respect to what makes them special varies according to nationality. But I would venture to say that there is one characteristic they all share and I propose that, even though they don't spend much time ruminating about strange coincidences, they recognize this one characteristic perfectly.

I'm speaking, of course, about guilt.

Maceta listens to the cretinous math lesson imparted by Mr. Reyna. Bored, he looks out the window and sees a group of nuns crossing the playground. He gets Lucía's attention and gestures for her to look outside. Lucía shrugs her shoulders. Maceta keeps looking, fascinated.

During recess, Maceta ignores his snack and his friends' games on the playground in favor of discreetly following the nuns, who are touring the campus accompanied by the principal. Maceta stays at just the right distance to overhear their conversation without being detected.

The way the nuns look is startling: they are very pale, blonde, blue-eyed. The Mother Superior speaks with a strong accent.

They are gringas.

"For us," she says, "it is a great pleasure to be able to share this gift with the children of your school."

"Of course, Sister," replies the principal with rare humility.

The group walks over to some large boxes stacked on the floor. Maceta watches everything from behind a wall.

"Here you have," explains the Mother Superior, "a donation made by the children of our nation, children of the very same age as your students here."

"Such kindness and generosity!" gushes the principal with an exaggerated bow.

Maceta listens carefully. Suddenly, Lucía appears behind him, surprising him.

"Hey!" she exclaims, and Maceta tells her to be quiet.

"What?" asks Lucía, conspiratorially.

"Our one condition," intones the Mother Superior, "that you will uphold, is that the books in these boxes be distributed fairly and at no cost among all of the students, in every grade."

"We would never have it any other way, Sister," says the principal, bowing with a reverence that even the nuns themselves find inappropriate.

"Amen," they all say with obvious discomfort.

Lucía and Maceta take off running.

Ah! Nothing like the chaos that ensues when a teacher leaves the classroom!

It's as if the devil himself enters our bodies and tries to tickle us to death. Especially when the teacher who leaves the classroom is an intractable disciplinarian like Reyna.

The roughhousing, the playacting, the dancing, the thunderous declamation of the choicest swear words, the showing off, it all becomes a race against the clock, a game of hot potato, a round of musical chairs, since no one knows when the teacher will come back, whom he will catch and in the act of doing what.

Fortunately for everyone, the teacher arrives carrying a heavy box that obstructs his vision and the students have enough time to quickly sit down and be quiet.

Reyna puts the box on top of his rotten desk and prepares to speak to the students.

"As you all know," he says, carefully enunciating each word, "I have dedicated my life to the scholastic profession. It is my vocation, my life's calling, a life I have given over completely to you, my beloved students. As a gesture of my sacrifice and of the selfless financial support bestowed by Molina, that tireless champion of justice and entrepreneurial leader in our community, I bring you these books . . ."

Lucía and Maceta exchange a look.

"Books of all shapes and sizes . . ."

Reyna opens the box and removes a book, triumphant.

"Written . . . in a language that is not ours, but filled with illustrations and pictures in lovely colors . . . And they're all for you! Yours . . . for a modest price. Come, come everyone, draw near, my children, take a look, choose the ones you want . . ."

The children start to get up from their seats and crowd around the box of books. Maceta and Lucía join the other curious children. They pull a few books out and share them around.

"Hey! Don't try to fool me. I've got my eye on you! Choose the ones you want and come talk to me to see what price we can agree on."

Lucía chooses an illustrated Brothers Grimm and begins to turn the pages as she walks back to her seat. Maceta looks at the books the other children choose, but he doesn't take one for himself. One little boy, trying to pull a heavy volume from the box, knocks several books to the floor.

"Careful!" shouts Reyna. "Be careful! Didn't I tell you to be careful? There are enough books for everyone."

Other children pick up the fallen books, all except one. This one catches Maceta's eye. It's called *Gaelic Mythology and Folklore*. Maceta picks it up.

Few are the people who can truly say that a book changed their lives. The majority of people who say it merely wish to establish that a book is very, very good and so they resort to that hackneyed hyperbole.

The book that Maceta picks up, *Gaelic Mythology and Folklore*, was not particularly good, but change his life it most certainly did.

Standing, alone, Maceta opens the book. He doesn't understand a single word, of course, but his face changes gradually from confusion to bewilderment . . . to the most complete astonishment. Like an echo, from far away, he gradually hears Reyna's voice bringing him back to reality.

"Maceta . . . Maceta . . . Maceta!"

Startled, Maceta unpeels his eyes from the book and looks at his teacher.

How much time has passed? Difficult to know for certain, but the other children are all already seated at their desks, and Maceta is alone, standing in front of the class, the book in his hands.

Everyone laughs. Reyna takes the book from him.

"Is this the one you want?" asks the teacher, looking the book over. Appraising it. "Five cents."

Maceta turns to look at his classmates, seeking out Lucía, who is sitting with the Brothers Grimm book she's just bought, looking back at him expectantly.

"I don't have any money, teacher," Maceta confesses. Reyna puts the book back in the box.

"Well, then, just pray to God that the book is still here when you get some."

The bell rings and the first to race out of the classroom is Maceta. Lucía is close on his heels, but suddenly, she stops.

"Maceta! Maceta!" she calls, intrigued, but Maceta has disappeared. Annoyed, Lucía goes back inside the classroom.

Reyna is tidying his desk and getting ready to leave for the day.

"Mr. Reyna . . ."

"Yes, Lucía?" says Reyna without looking at her.

"Can I . . . can I change books?"

"You don't like yours and now you want another one?"

"I want the one Maceta had."

Reyna looks at her in irritation, considers her offer and looks for the book inside the box. He takes her book and assesses them both.

"Five more cents," he decrees.

Lucía thinks it over, a little disappointed. After a brief pause, she takes a small change purse from her pocket and pays. Reyna gives her Maceta's book and keeps the Brothers Grimm.

A fool is a fool is a fool.

And a fool in love is even worse.

Lucía lies in wait for Maceta who, in turn, lies in wait for the custodian, sitting on a little wall near the toolshed. When the custodian arrives and goes inside the shed, Maceta approaches him and, after a few seconds, the custodian gives him a small shovel. Lucía can see, by his gestures, that the custodian is warning Maceta to be careful with the shovel and to return it.

Maceta runs happily away.

Without going to look for her first.

The one who breaks your heart most completely is the one who knows you most completely.

Lucía walks over to a secluded bench on the playground and sits down. She calmly and thoroughly flips through the pages of the book. Within them she finds colorful illustrations accompanied by scattered text in a language she doesn't understand. She sees a druid, a mandala, a warrior with a painted face . . .

Maceta, carrying his backpack, lunchbox and shovel, starts down his usual route home: he goes in the opposite direction from which he came, crosses a small and filthy stream, climbs up the bank and takes the private path that runs along the chain-link fence that surrounds the golf course.

He runs toward the fallen tree trunk, sets everything down, sits and waits.

Lucía turns a page and pauses, looking at the book with a perplexed expression.

The page shows a rainbow. The next series of images shows a boy running toward the place where the rainbow ends and meets the ground; the boy bent over and digging with a shovel; the boy unearthing a pot brimming with gold coins.

In the final vignette we see a little man, a dwarf, hairy and bearded—fierce and apelike and dressed in ill-fitting clothes, a lunatic not that very different from the one who prowls the streets of her neighborhood, muttering constantly about a war and some soldiers and a special operation and a woman—with an expression of rage on his face, upset because the boy has stolen his treasure.

Lucía has no way of knowing it at that moment, but that little bearded man she is looking at is a *leprechaun*, a word derived from the Middle Irish *luchrupán*, which, in turn, comes from the ancient Irish *luchorpán*, and which means, quite simply, "dwarf." Leprechauns are a type of fairy and, as such, they belong to the small nobility, those mischievous beings who live in the folds of reality, who concede wishes (in their own way, obviously), collect trinkets (made of gold and precious stones, of course) and who were known by the magical name of *Tuatha Dé Danann* in Gaelic Ireland.

I wonder if beings from such far-off latitudes can stand how hot it is here.

Lucía furrows her brow, trying to understand. A dark shadow moves over her and she looks up. It's the Mother Superior, who looks at her, smiling. After a moment, the nun extends her long, bony index finger and drops it atop the rainbow pictured in the pages of the book. Lucía looks at the finger and then at the nun, who says slowly:

"Rainbow . . . Rain. Bow. *Rainbow.*"

Lucía doesn't take her eyes off the nun as she repeats:

"Reinbou."

"That's right!" exclaims the Mother Superior, satisfied. "Good job!"

The Mother Superior leaves, her habit waving in the breeze. Lucía remains alone, looking at the book.

The sprinklers on the golf course come on. A beautiful rainbow appears. Maceta stands up, throws the shovel over the fence and then, with some difficulty, climbs over himself, landing on the other side. He runs toward the rainbow, but the rainbow grows farther away with equal speed, and Maceta never reaches it.

"What on Earth?"

Maceta reasons that the rainbow is a surly creature and he cannot approach it so abruptly.

Slowly, then.

Step by step, Maceta manages to reach the place where the rainbow meets the ground, drenching himself in the water from the sprinklers and the seven primary colors.

He begins to dig.

After a good long while, Maceta uses his hands to remove a final fistful of earth and sticks his face down into the moderately sized hole he has made in the lawn. He gazes at his discovery in silence, making an effort to decipher it. He bends to pick it up.

1965

Puro emerges from the moderately sized hole. Inma helps him out and replaces the boards that conceal the hollow in which she hides her contraband, and puts her little wooden table back on top of the boards.

Puro sits on the floor, looks at the twins, smiles at them affably. Then he looks at Inma, standing in front of him, hands on her hips. Inma looks at him with resignation. She looks away after a moment and walks toward the cookstove.

"Do you want coffee?"

Puro nods his head. Inma starts bustling around the stove, while Puro moves over toward the kerosene lamp. A book lies open on the rickety wooden table.

"What are you reading?" inquires the fugitive, and just when he is about to see for himself, Inma beats him to it, closes the book and takes it away.

"The Bible," says Inma and puts the book on a high shelf. She hands Puro a mug of coffee. She's made herself a cup too. They sit down facing each other in silence.

"You have to leave," decrees Inma after two or three sips. Puro, caught off guard by the order, stands to go. Inma stops him.

"Not now, you idiot!" she says. "They're still out there."

Puro sits down again. They sit in silence once more. Puro looks around, taking in Inma's circumstances.

"I didn't know that you were living here," he says and regrets it immediately.

"Here? Or like this?" Inma spits at him, and Puro understands that his regret was premonitory. Inma shrugs.

"What happened to the house?" insists Puro, digging his own grave.

"The house? Your little war stopped by the house."

Why don't I just shut up? thinks Puro.

"We lost it when they killed Papá," explains Inma, taking pity on the revolutionary's clumsiness. But the compassion she feels for him evaporates as she speaks the words. She stares at Puro and raises her cup in a toast.

"To the cause."

"No one told me," says Puro, dismayed.

Inma stands abruptly.

"What a shame," she says. "One less opportunity to play the hero. You would have come to the rescue immediately, I expect."

Inma moves to the stove and throws the dregs from her cup into the embers. She scrubs the mug with water from a bucket.

"Rinse that out when you're done and go lie down."

Inma puts out the kerosene lamp. She settles down on the floor, next to her sisters, but before lying down, she props herself up on one elbow.

"In this world," she sermonizes, "everyone ultimately does what they have to do in order to survive. That's what I'm doing. That's what these two are going to do too. Stop dreaming . . . Get it out of your head that you can fix people's lives. You can't. Not today, not ever."

Inma curls up on the floor. Puro sits in the darkness, cup in hand. He takes small sips. Crosses his legs.

Inma stretches out.

"Your welcome expires at first light," she announces.

1976

Maceta is walking home; he carries an old bicycle chain in his hands.

In his notebook he has written:

> **LINKED FACTORS.** *Not one is the first and not one is the last. If the order does not alter the product, then the order does not exist. The product is a type of necklace without a clasp.*

He runs into Don Chago along the way, squatting with Jacinto in front of his tricycle cart.

"It's very short, Chago," concludes Jacinto. "You have to find the right one. Or, to make this one work, we have to cut or flatten these tubes and weld them to get closer to the cogs . . . It'll be just like from the factory."

Chago looks at him with the expression of a person who cannot believe his own ears.

"That will take too long, Jacinto," laments Chago, "and I've already lost a whole day of work looking for a replacement."

"Good afternoon, Don Chago. Good afternoon, Don Jacinto."

"Good afternoon, Maceta," the men say in unison. Chago notices the chain in Maceta's hands.

"Maceta, mijo, where did you find that chain?"

"I dug it up. In the rainbow field."

Chago and Jacinto look at each other, perplexed. They've known Maceta since he was a baby, but they still have trouble getting used to the things he comes up with.

"Uh huh . . . ," says Chago.

"But it isn't a chain. They are . . . Well. I'll give them to you, if you want them," says Maceta, handing the chain to Chago. "I already wrote it down in my notebook, so . . . it's all yours."

"Thank you, Maceta."

"You're welcome, Don Chago."

Maceta goes on his way. Jacinto tries the chain.

It fits perfectly.

"I'll be damned . . . ," he says. "It's the perfect size, Chago. We're done. It just needs a little grease and you're back in business."

Chago looks stunned. He looks at Maceta walking happily away toward his house. He looks back at the chain.

"How could it . . . ?"

➤

Clarisa and Melisa are getting ready for the night. One dries the other's hair as she does her makeup in a fragment of broken mirror. Then they change places.

"Hi, Maceta!" they say together.

"Hi."

"Your mom's inside," says Clarisa. "Go say hi to her."

Maceta enters the shack. Inma is inside with Raúl, feeding the baby in total silence. It would appear that they've just finished one of their discussions. Raúl looks at Maceta in disgust.

"Hello, mami."

"Hello, mijo, come give me a kiss."

Maceta drops his backpack to the floor and kisses his mother.

"I'm a little bit hungry," he tells her in a low voice, but Raúl hears him.

"Why don't we just cook up that uniform of yours?" he says.

Maceta and Inma look at Raúl: Maceta surprised, Inma annoyed.

"Whaddaya say, Doctor Maceta? You in the mood for a little book soup? A pencil sandwich?"

What a jackass. I know, right?

But be patient, Christmas has almost arrived for that suckling pig.

Maceta, dear little soul, finds the bitter sarcasm funny and he laughs. Raúl gets to his feet, looming, and knocks him to the floor with a slap to the face. Inma screams and, the baby in her arms, stands defiantly between Maceta and Raúl, who clearly means to continue punishing his stepson.

Chago, standing in the doorframe, coughs to announce his presence; in his hands, some plastic bags.

"Greetings, forgive me . . . May I come in?"

"Of course, Chago . . . come in," says Inma, not taking her eyes off Raúl.

"Thank you, Inma. How's everything going?"

Inma answers with a nod, not saying a word.

"And the baby? How is she?"

"Healthy and getting bigger every day."

Chago looks at Raúl, whom he has ignored up until this point.

"Raúl."

Raúl doesn't answer, but, after all, Chago isn't expecting a response, and he returns his attention to Inma.

"Anyway . . . here are some taro roots, they're really good, and also . . ."

"Chago, that's not necessary."

"Let me finish . . ."

"I don't want them, Chago," says Inma, offended. "We haven't sunk so low as to have to live off our neighbors' charity. Thank you."

"I'm sure you haven't," explains Chago, "but they're not for you."

Inma looks confused.

"They're for my partner, Maceta, who today became . . . an investor in my business."

Chago looks at Maceta and winks at him. Inma looks at him too, not understanding.

"And partners lend a hand when one's needed."

Chago leaves the bags on the floor, next to the door.

"I'll leave them here and I'll go tell the girls to light the fire in the cookstove. These taro roots are really good, pure starch . . ."

Chago is about to leave, but he pauses in the door.

"I'll be stopping by every afternoon to bring you whatever I don't sell during the day," Chago tells Maceta. "How does that sound, partner?"

Maceta nods.

"Good luck at school tomorrow!"

Chago leaves. Inma smiles at Maceta, who returns the smile, and then she proceeds to look at Raúl with an expression of unsurpassable contempt. Raúl leaves the house, smashing things as he goes.

Inma draws Maceta to her and hugs him.

The second treasure the rainbow reveals to Maceta on the golf course is a number eight billiard ball.

An eight ball . . . a special one.

It is much larger than normal and it's full of liquid. It's not completely round, but has a flat side that serves as a base, in which there is also a small transparent window. Every time Maceta turns the base upward, a polyhedron floats through the liquid—which turns out to be blue—and knocks against the little window. The faces of the polyhedron present a different message each time.

Maceta stops by Simón and Tomás's shop.

"Simón, my son, drop it. No one wants that gum. Let's stick with the other brand."

"Papá, I'm telling you. This is the one they're asking for. The other stores are already carrying it. We're the only shop in the neighborhood that doesn't have it."

"What does it say there? 'Duble Buble?'"

"Double Bubble," says Simón, his pronunciation almost perfect. Not for nothing does he have a Dominican York girlfriend.

"You see, some stupid thing impossible to pronounce."

"And do you have to pronounce it right in order to know what they're asking us for? What difference does it make? The way you just said it is how the kids are asking for it in all the other shops, and the shopkeepers aren't throwing a fit saying they don't know what they're asking for."

"Hello, Don Tomás and Simón," says Maceta, crouching down in front of the debaters to tie his shoes.

"Hi, Maceta," reply father and son.

"Simón," says Tomás, determined to have the last word, "let me put it to you this way. That thick gum costs me three cents more, so we have to sell it for more. Are people really going to buy more expensive gum just because it's popular with the kids?"

The eight ball rolls out of Maceta's half-tipped-over backpack toward Tomás's feet. Tomás picks it up and, together with Simón, examines it. Against the transparent little window, the following message appears: *Signs point to yes.*

Simón opens his eyes wide and gives a little jump.

"Ha!" he exclaims in triumph. "Look at that!"

Maceta stands up and looks at the pair of them. Tomás shakes the ball.

"If I don't sell that gum," the shopkeeper specifies, "will the competition get ahead of me?"

As the pair consults the little window, the following advice emerges from the bluish water: *You may rely on it.*

Simón takes the eight ball from his father, shakes it, and asks: "Am I always right or what?"

The answer: *Don't count on it.*

Now it's Tomás's turn to laugh, exultant.

"Ah . . . ," says Maceta, raising his chin at the dawning of comprehension. "That's what it's for!"

Tomás and Simón try to give the eight ball back to Maceta, but Maceta won't accept it.

"I think you two can get better use out of it," he says.

Minutes later, sitting on a tall stool at the counter, devouring the cookie and Malta Morena that Tomás and Simón have given him, Maceta writes in his journal.

> **PORTABLE UMPIRE.** *Mysterious object that answers important questions and offers instant mediation in any argument. The secret is in the blue-colored water, doubtless a mysterious liquid being with wondrous abilities.*

The next day, Maceta arrives on his street with a basketball hoop.

Maceta has never seen a basketball court in all his life, much less a hoop like the one he's carrying, and so he doesn't have the slightest idea what it is.

Neither do Jacinto and Eneida's many sons, who scamper about, shove one another, fight, cry, get bored, make life impossible for their parents, get scolded, punished and spanked by said parents, only to begin the cycle all over again.

But Jacinto recognizes the hoop and knows what it's for.

"Maceta," Jacinto calls out. "Come here."

Maceta obeys.

"What's that?"

"Today's treasure."

"Uh huh . . ."

"It's a steel circle," says Maceta, showing the hoop to Jacinto. "But, of course, it can't be only a steel circle. It must be something else and I'm not recognizing it."

"Maceta," explains Jacinto, taking the hoop from his hands, "this is . . . Let's see."

Jacinto motions for Maceta to follow him.

They find four nails in Chago's house and Lidio loans them a hammer from his shop. A neighbor, reading Jacinto's intention, calls out that, without a backboard, they might as well throw that hoop in the trash, which another neighbor overhears, promptly furnishing a thick sheet of plywood that he had lying around. A can of black paint appears from somewhere, and Lidio shouts at Maceta to go find a paintbrush.

Olivero, Jacintico, Juan Matías, Garibaldi and William Sócrates, all exactly one year in age apart from the next, quit annoying their mother and join the group of men who have gathered around Jacinto, who is painting a black square on the bottom edge of the piece of plywood. Someone brings more nails, tie wire, another hammer. A ladder appears.

After a great deal of discussion about regulation height, after much hammering and reinforcing with wire, Jacinto, his sons, Maceta, and the rest of the men who helped with the operation look up at the basketball hoop they have erected on a sturdy light post.

Someone—most likely the same man who had earlier suggested they toss the hoop in the trash; there's a guy like him in every neighborhood—shouts, unseen, that the hoop turned out so great that probably, if they stare at it long enough, it will give birth to a ball. But from his store, Simón bounces a ball toward the crowd, an old Spalding he's just inflated, a gift from Yolanda, his girlfriend, when she came to visit last year for Semana Santa.

Olivero, Jacinto and Eneida's eldest son, intercepts the ball with ease.

He's never dribbled a ball before in his life, but that's exactly what he does now, before passing it to Jacintico who does the same, then passes it to Juan Matías, who does the same and passes it to Garibaldi, who adds a dribble through his legs and passes it to William Sócrates who, not thinking twice about the impulse he feels upon holding the ball in his hands, throws it up toward the hoop and scores a basket.

The rest is history.

Last year, Olivero was inducted into the Hall of Fame and he sent us that great photo that you two keep in your bedroom.

Jacintico retired in November due to a knee injury, but he's happy: he's been wanting to spend more time with his family for a while now. Juan Matías and Garibaldi followed in their footsteps with the Chicago Bulls, and William Sócrates just signed with the Lakers.

Go ahead and laugh at the next person who tells you that a book changed their life.

Maceta discovered many treasures in the weeks to come, and every one of them had the virtue of transforming someone's day. Many of the beneficiaries of his gifts needed no more than that: a little push on a single day, a jumpstart to their battery just that once, for someone to apply the necessary spark. After that, they'd tend the fire, feed the flames, stoke the embers all on their own.

And as the residents' personal outlooks begin to change, so too, does the neighborhood begin to change.

Maceta's gifts, needless to say, were just pieces of junk. At least to the untrained eye. And possibly they were junk, it's true, but miraculously *opportune* junk. But opportune junk is an oxymoron. Opportune junk ceases to be junk and turns into something else. It turns into what Maceta has always insisted it is: treasure.

Maceta's treasures were of all different sorts. Maceta never settled for conventional explanations or for the commonly

accepted names for things. Rather, he waited to gather suffi-
cient data to allow him to penetrate the essence of the treasures
that the rainbow revealed to him, without fail, on the golf
course. Sometimes a single careful observation of the item and
its workings was all he needed. Other times he had to wait to
examine the effects of an object upon one or more people, or
to study the way in which someone put it to use. Because Maceta
was interested exclusively in the spirit of the thing, not in the
thing itself.

At first glance, for example, the vinyl disc that he receives
from the earth's bowels is clearly an old Benny Moré LP, perfectly
preserved inside its record sleeve. But Maceta would never pro-
fane his notebook by writing *LP*. It's not until he observes what
Don Jorge Aníbal and his band of little old men and women *do*
with it, and the *effect* it has on them, that he opens his journal
and records:

REVOLVING HAPPINESS. *Black circle that contains*
happiness and memories. In order to release them, it is
necessary to spin it on a special machine.

Likewise, the flute that the Arab upholsterers at the end of the
street ask him for, which, expertly played by the aged patriarch,
transforms the standoffish foreigners into lighthearted dancers
clapping their hands, is less a flute than a *Party Concentrate.* "Just
add air," is all Maceta notes in his inventory.

The bird feeder he gave to Mercedes, the seamstress, is a *Bird*
Multiplier; the little Saint Christopher figurine that Alberto, the

taxi driver, asked him for, is a *Force Field for Automobiles*; the antenna that Lidio used to repair his transistor radio, the prior explanation of its function, is a *Perch for Voices* . . .

And so on.

Maceta's treasures also had a residual effect.

Let me explain.

Jorge Aníbal's *revolving happiness* summoned others, rescued by other neighbors or acquired in other parts of the city, in such a way that the old folks' collection grew. And not only the collection; the number of people who gathered together at Jorge Aníbal's house grew as well. It became necessary to establish a schedule. Then, rules. Later, they began to charge membership fees, and the gathering became a club. With the membership fee money, they bought a new hi-fi system and more records, and they rented out event spaces for parties. Many were the solitary widowers and abandoned widows who met at these soirées, never again to be parted.

One of the grateful who found a girlfriend in his old age was Don Goyo, the cantankerous gardener. A woman from Higüey with whom he, almost by accident, had danced a Cuban *son* in Jorge Aníbal's carport, moved in with him. From that moment on, it became common knowledge that any neighbor who took an empty jar, tin can, flowerpot, planter, bucket or bin over to Don Goyo's house was a neighbor who'd leave with a cutting from a wisteria, clock vine, golden trumpet, Maltese cross, hibiscus, bougainvillea, angel's trumpet, shrimp plant or lantana. In no time at all, the neighborhood filled with color.

Happiness makes people feel like giving. And planting.

And flying.

Visiting Mercedes's house to drop off items to be mended or sewn became a pleasant experience, as the customer was instantly surrounded by doves, bananaquits, nightingales, kingbirds and palm chats. When Mercedes saw that the birdseed wasn't enough to satisfy all her winged visitors and that the kingbirds bullied the peaceful doves and the nightingales frightened the bananaquits, she had two additional bird feeders built. The air around her shack now hummed with fluttering wings and birdsong, and flocks of broad-billed todys, greater Antillean pewees, village weavers, thrushes, tanagers, nightjars and grackles joined the more regular visitors.

In the evenings, when the commotion died down, a timid black-whiskered vireo would approach and ring in the hour with its song.

Soon, Mercedes couldn't keep up with the volume of work she received and she had to hire help. Later she left the neighborhood and bought a shop in a bustling shopping center.

And so on.

One day, Maceta comes home with a mirror.

It's an unusual mirror. It's not made of glass, but rather, of metal, and it has a heavily ornamented metallic frame.

It might be a tray . . . but it's square and it doesn't have any handles.

It's a mirror.

It's a mirror for the common folk. Maceta still doesn't know what he'll write in his notebook.

The clientele at his aunts' improvised open-air "beauty salon" has increased, in part because the women and young ladies who take their mending to Mercedes take advantage of the opportunity to have their hair washed and dried before heading back home.

Maceta greets his aunts, who kiss and fawn over him as always. When he manages to detach himself, he walks to the tamarind tree, takes down the old, broken mirror and hangs up the one he's just found.

"Oh, Maceta!" exclaims Clarisa. "What's that?"

Melisa comes over.

"Thank you!" says Melisa, peering at it closely. The mirror is cloudy, dusty.

"Wait," says Clarisa. "Let's wipe it down with a rag."

Clarisa holds the mirror while Melisa polishes it with a piece of damp cloth.

And, little by little, the twins' reflection emerges on the metallic surface.

Clarisa and Melisa appear hypnotized, enthralled, absorbed by what they see. They are so used to seeing themselves fragmented in the old, cracked mirror that now that they can see themselves as they really are, they feel as though they are seeing two strangers.

Two strangers of indescribable beauty, of captivating hauteur, of overwhelming insolence, of unshakeable disposition, of highly dangerous audacity.

The reflection awakens pleasant memories in them. They look at one another. It's a long look of understanding, of decision. They don't need to say a single word; everything has been said.

"Yocelyn," calls Clarisa, "come get your hair dried."

Yocelyn heeds her call and comes to sit in front of the mirror.

"Sobeida," calls Melisa, "come get your hair washed."

Sobeida obeys.

And the women keep on coming.

Maceta writes in his notebook:

MIRROR MIRROR. *Smooth surface that returns a reflection without interference or sound, showing whoever uses it the best possible version of themselves.*

The last rainbow Maceta chases is the most skittish of all. He runs after it across almost the entire golf course, but the rainbow always moves away from him. Before he realizes it, he's far away; he's lost sight of the chain-link fence and he's close to the far opposite end of the golf course.

Only then does the rainbow slow down, and Maceta can see it touch down on the other side of the fence, in a thicket of weeds and underbrush. He hesitates for a moment, but finally decides to go over to the other side to investigate. He scales the chain-link fence (he's an expert by now), works his way into the dense vegetation and advances with difficulty through the thicket until he comes to a clearing.

In the clearing there is a small shack, built from scraps of wood, cardboard and zinc sheeting. Behind the shack there is a small, wooded hill overflowing with an avalanche of garbage. The rainbow ends just above the shack.

A rock falls near Maceta. Surprised, Maceta looks around and discovers Loco Abril, standing like a ghost among the trees, looking at him with his empty gaze, rigid as a corpse.

Rigid until he suddenly and nimbly bends over, grabs another rock, and throws it. The rock lands very close to the boy's feet, which, even so, remain planted.

Maceta thinks that Loco Abril is not so far away and that, even though he's crazy, it couldn't be true that he has such terrible aim. If he had wanted to nail him with a rock, he would have; nailing passersby with rocks is what Loco Abril does best.

Conclusion: Loco Abril doesn't want to hit him, but rather, to warn him.

They stand like that for a good long while, looking at one another. Maceta is the first to retreat. He climbs the chain-link fence again and retraces his steps.

Loco Abril goes inside his shack.

1965

They beat Oviedo bald, to use Inma's famous phrase, inherited from her father, Pancho Carmona, who also used to say *they whupped him from nipples to nuts,* to make it clear that someone had been beaten thoroughly, in great detail, and for a very long time.

As I was saying, they caught Oviedo and strung him up by his wrists in an old, abandoned warehouse. His feet just barely touched the floor, which gave Oviedo the illusion that he could stand. So the prisoner constantly tried, and failed, to hold himself up, hurting his hands, dislocating his shoulders and involuntarily stretching out his solar plexus, a situation that puts the captive in a vulnerable position and greatly facilitates the effective application of body blows by whips, sticks, belts, fists, feet.

The light from a high bulb illuminates the space.

Oviedo's face is one big, bloody mess, and another blow lands on that bloody mess, more or less in the place where you'd guess his nose to be.

The prisoner is surrounded by soldiers, but they're not marines; these are homegrown soldiers, members of the glorious Armed Forces of the Dominican Republic. The one beating him is Sergeant Subero, who takes advantage of the opportunity to educate his boys.

"When the subject is as you see this one now," he pontificates, "don't hit him as hard as you did at the beginning, because you don't want him to faint. The objective now is to hurt the injuries he already has, and you don't need to hit so hard in order to do that. Also, it's important not to exhaust yourself. Observe: Do you see his nose? Completely broken. This guy's nose will be crooked for the rest of his life. I think this cheekbone is also broken. Do you see? And that hurts like a son of a bitch. His eyes are fucked; he can't see past his own eyelashes. He might have lost this eye; I'm not sure. We'll know when the swelling goes down. Do you see this ear? That's called cauliflower ear. Also permanent. He won't be deaf, but he won't hear anything anyone whispers to him in that ear. When the order is to interrogate, always try not to break any extremities; we need the captive to be able to walk, or to sign a statement, or to lead us somewhere. Leaving the prisoner crippled means more work for us. When the order is to punish before killing, break whatever you like, since the last stop will be a bullet to the back of the head and a ditch. In this present case . . . well, it's not exactly clear if we're interrogating or punishing, but you already know that the Yankees work in mysterious ways. For now, we can't let this poor bastard die on us."

César Antonio Subero Rodríguez achieved the rank of sergeant first class and was honorably discharged four years after the clash with the constitutionalist insurgents. He never, however, stopped collecting his E7 pay grade salary, and even today, as a Catholic priest of an affluent parish in the capital and spiritual leader of the adjoining school, he continues to receive his compensation.

A feminine form observes from the shadows, leaning against the wall, smoking a cigarette. Off to the side stand a barrel of water, a table, and a small electric generator.

That's for later.

Subero hits Oviedo again, this time in the stomach, three, four, five hard punches. Subero pants as he walks in a circle around Oviedo. He stops in front of him. He bends over and studies Oviedo's face up close. He turns around and addresses his audience in a whisper.

"And never, ever, ever forget to combine physical punishment with psychological intimidation and mental abuse."

Subero holds out his arm and a soldier places a hammer in his hand. He smiles at Oviedo as he holds the hammer under Oviedo's nose so he can smell it.

"Make it clear to the prisoner," he says, still in a whisper, "that the worst is always yet to come."

Subero once again turns to face Oviedo, who has heard the sergeant's lesson perfectly. He slowly raises his face, looks Subero in the eye . . . and spits a glob of saliva and blood in his face.

Subero closes his eyes in disgust, wipes his face with his shirt-sleeve, and winds up on a hammer swing that will cave Oviedo's head in.

A woman's voice thunders in the empty warehouse.

"Stop!"

Sergeant Subero halts.

"Leave us alone," booms the voice, authoritative and with a hint of impatience.

Subero and the rest of the soldiers obey like robots and walk out of the building. Oviedo is alone.

Major McCollum emerges from the shadows. She throws the cigarette butt to the floor and crushes it under her military boot. She comes and stands in front of Oviedo. A slightly bloody bandage covers her right eye.

"Remember me?" she says and points to her injured eye. "Thanks for the little gift . . ."

Oviedo swallows. McCollum looks around.

"Because I remember you."

McCollum walks around Oviedo, taking her time. She leans in close to his ear.

"I trusted you."

A shudder runs through Oviedo.

"And what does that have to do with anything?" he mumbles, not expecting to be heard. But McCollum hears him perfectly and smacks him hard across the face.

Oviedo spits out a tooth and starts to laugh.

"But," he says, "why did you do that?"

The major looks at him with barely contained rage.

"That was a lot of money . . ." she clarifies. Then a look of tenderness comes over her. She approaches Oviedo and caresses his deformed face.

Then McCollum reaches into her jacket pocket for her pack of cigarettes, takes one out and places it between Oviedo's lips. She pulls the matches out of her other pocket.

"What the fuck were you thinking?" she says, lighting the cigarette for him. "What the hell are you guys going to do now? Take it to a pawnshop? How do you plan to liquidate it? It's not so easy, at least not for people like you. And not here, in this pigsty that you call a country."

"I don't have it . . ." mutters Oviedo, letting the cigarette drop. McCollum bursts out laughing.

"Who, then? Puro? Don't fuck with me, Oviedo. You have it. And you're going to tell me where it is."

Oviedo just breathes, with extreme difficulty.

McCollum approaches him, lifts his face. A tear escapes from her left eye. The bloodstain spreads across the bandage covering her right eye.

"I loved you," she says, holding back a sob.

Oviedo looks at her, or he tries to.

"That doesn't make sense," he says, mercilessly.

McCollum's face ignites and turns hard. The major releases Oviedo's head; he lacks the strength to hold it upright and lets it fall against his chest. McCollum takes three steps back and calls out into the dark warehouse:

"Boys!"

A group of five men emerges from the shadows and comes into the light; they surround Oviedo. They're white, with golden hair and enormous muscles that undulate beneath their shirts. Vikings in marine uniforms.

"You see? Those guys who were here a while ago, your countrymen," says McCollum, lighting another cigarette, "they were just toying with you. No matter what they believe, no matter what they say, somewhere deep, deep, deep inside themselves, they consider you part of their team. Born in the same country, fellow compatriot and blah blah blah . . ."

McCollum gestures at the five men surrounding Oviedo.

"But these sons of bitches . . ." McCollum says, laughing. "These sons of bitches see you and the only thing they see is a disgusting goddamn Negro."

McCollum exhales a thick cloud of smoke.

"That's how it is. And they're veeeery good at what they do."

McCollum gives Oviedo time to understand just exactly what he's stepped in.

"These guys aren't like those rookies you had in here before. These guys will fuck up your life, and fuck it up good; so much that you'll end up wishing they'd kill you . . . But . . . they don't kill you."

McCollum draws near to Oviedo.

"These guys will crush your bones."

McCollum presses her index finger into Oviedo's chest.

"These guys will pull out your intestines and eat them in front of you. Believe me, I've seen them do it."

McCollum takes a drag from her cigarette.

"I don't want to frighten you . . . It's just to inform you."

McCollum puts the pack of cigarettes away in one pocket and the matches in another. As she's saying this last part, two of the men are arranging an assorted array of instruments of torture on the table. Terror disfigures Oviedo's face.

"The important thing," McCollum explains, "is to get it out of your head that you're going to leave here alive. At the very least, I can assure you that the Oviedo you and I both know will not. I can assure you of that. And so, for the last time, tell me what I want to hear, because if I don't hear what I want to hear . . . I'm going to sic the dogs on you."

Oviedo looks at the newcomers. He speaks, his tone sheepish.

"Puro . . . Puro has it."

McCollum closes her eyes, disappointed, opens them again, begins to walk away.

"Puro has it," Oviedo begs.

The five men prepare to go to work. Panic overcomes Oviedo. McCollum keeps walking away.

"Puro has it!" Oviedo screams in desperation.

And that's how the Yankees created Loco Abril.

Puro is sitting on the floor with Clarisa and Melisa, leafing through a newspaper. Inma is still deeply asleep.

"Cea . . ." Clarisa reads.

"Very good," Puro encourages her. "Keep going. Uh-huh. 'Cea . . .'"

"Cea . . . se . . . Cease."

"Your turn," Puro says to Melisa.

"Fi . . . re."

"That's it!"

Both twins tentatively chew over the final word.

"Broken!" they exclaim at last.

"Very good. 'Ceasefire broken.' Excellent."

Inma moves in her sleep, rolls over, turning her back to Puro and the girls. Puro puts his index finger to his lips, urging the twins to be quiet.

"Do you like my sister?" Melisa asks in a conspiratorial whisper. Clarisa laughs quietly. Puro smiles.

"Your sister and I grew up together," Puro tells them. "We did everything together. But she got really bad grades in school."

The girls cover their mouths, trying to contain their laughter.

"I helped her, but . . ." Puro says with a gesture of resignation. "It was a different story in the schoolyard. When the big kids harassed me or tried to steal my money or destroy my books or school supplies, she would grab them and . . ."

Puro mimes punching someone. The girls can scarcely control the laughter trapped inside their mouths.

"And then?" Clarisa asks. Puro sighs.

But Inma, whose back is to them, is awake and she's listening very, very carefully.

"Then . . ." Puro continues. "Then I went to the university; I graduated. Your sister kept helping your dad. She loved him very much . . . and so did I."

Inma smiles. She coughs, faking that she's just waking up. Puro and the girls gather themselves and fall silent, as if they hadn't been saying or doing anything. Inma stands, stretches.

Puro looks at her appreciatively. He can't help it. If he could have helped it, there'd be no story. Besides which, the body that mamagüela, at that time, was letting go to waste wasn't easy to ignore, not by men or women or by the sun, the wind, the rain or the cobblestones on the streets. And especially when all she had on was a threadbare camisole that was too small for her.

But that was the least of it.

Here was a man running for his life.

Hidden in a shack on the edge of a garbage dump while outside, soldiers from the most powerful army in the world are swarming, bent on finding and killing him . . . But all it takes is for him to sneak a peek at Inma's backside, and Puro no longer knows what day of the week it is; he is flooded with an impossible-to-define sensation—you'd have to be a man to truly know what it is—and his survival no longer occupies first place on his brain's list of priorities. And that sensation convinces Puro that he's invincible and, instead of calculating how he's going to escape that place, he invests his neurons' efforts in imagining what it will feel like to grab those two masses lifting the edge of the camisole.

Men are idiots, my daughters. And this is good and bad in equal measure.

Inma goes about her business as though Puro weren't there, although she knows perfectly well that he is there. With her back to Puro, she lights the cookstove and starts the coffee.

Inma is a woman and, like all women, she knows exactly when someone's looking at her ass and with what level of intensity. And I'm telling you, what Inma does is she arches her lower back to lift her backside a little higher so Puro can get an even better look at it.

Yes, you heard right.

This woman, who is harboring a fugitive being hunted by the invading army of a superpower, endangering the lives of her little sisters as well as her own, tilts her tailbone in an unnecessary and uncomfortable way while she makes the coffee, with the sole purpose of getting inside the head of the man looking at her from behind.

We women are also idiots, my daughters. We women are also idiots.

It's as if these two people had been kidnapped by their own bodies and put on autopilot. And that autopilot doesn't give a damn about Yankees, or the country, or death.

"Good morning," says Inma.

"Morning," says Puro.

Inma steps behind a screen to get dressed.

"What's in that bag?" asks Inma, whose silhouette Puro can see perfectly.

At Inma's question, Puro looks at his suitcase and it's as if he's just now suddenly remembered its existence. He pulls it over, opens it and looks inside.

His face freezes. A mask of total astonishment. He starts laughing, but it's a tragic laugh, a cheap imitation of weeping. Inma emerges, dressed, her hair fixed up.

"Tell me."

Puro closes the suitcase and considers his answer.

"Peace."

Inma gives him a condescending look and bursts out laughing. She looks inside the suitcase too and says to Puro in a low voice:

"If you say so. But I know it by a different name."

Puro shakes his head in resignation and smiles. Inma walks over to the hidey-hole in the floor, moves the little wooden table aside, lifts the boards that cover the opening, lies down on the floor and reaches her arm inside. She takes out two cloth bags and covers the hole again.

"Girls."

Each girl grabs a bag.

"You, go to Casandra's. Thirty pesos, no more, no less. If she doesn't want to give it to you, or she doesn't have it, leave and go to Don Arturo's. You, go to Ramiro's shop. Sixty pesos, and be firm with him, but if he argues a lot and won't give in, go down to fifty, but that's all. Get going."

The twins leave. Inma stands facing Puro.

"Keep an eye on the coffee and serve yourself," she orders. "I'm going to take a little walk. If the coast is clear, I'll come back and you're out of here, and I mean quickly."

"Yes, General."

Inma doesn't like the joke and she leaves in a huff. Puro is alone in the shack.

He goes to the cookstove, where he makes a cup of coffee, waiting patiently as it drips through the sock-like cloth filter. He takes his cup and sits down in the little chair in which Inma had been reading the night before. He drinks unhurriedly, with a worried look on his face that suddenly clears, giving way to an expression of surprise, as if he were remembering something. He sets his coffee on the table, stands and walks straight to the tall shelf where Inma put the book she'd been reading when he blew into the house like a gust of wind in the middle of the night. He finds it. He holds it in his hands: *Essay on Inequality among Dominicans*, by Puro Maceta Gómez.

Puro laughs. He caresses the cover of his doctoral thesis. Print run of just five hundred copies. Every one of them sold and the book now banned. *And just look where one turns up,* thinks Puro.

Inma enters the shack and closes the door. Seeing what Puro's holding, her face becomes a paragon of unspeakable fury. She walks over to him, snatches the book and puts it back where it was. She stands in front of him and levels her gaze at him. She crosses her arms.

"The coast is clear," she says. Puro looks at her and, after a brief moment, he moves away, picks up his suitcase and heads for the door. When he's just about to open it . . .

"No," sighs Inma. Puro looks at her, confused.

"Are there soldiers or no?" he asks.

"No," replies Inma.

"So, can I go?"

"Yes."

Puro starts to open the door.

"No," Inma says again.

Puro closes the door, turns around and sets the suitcase on the floor. Inma is dying of embarrassment, looking everywhere except at Puro.

"You can go and you can also stay . . . ," she says.

Puro, palomo extraordinaire, is completely confused. Inma finally looks at him, with an expression of pity and frustration.

"I seriously have no idea why all those people listen to you. Leader of what?"

"Inma . . ."

Inma pounces on him, exasperated.

"Why do I always have to do everything? Why is it always me!"

The last word is barely out of her mouth and she's kissing him with wild abandon, her tongue plunging into Puro's mouth. They start to undress, hastily and clumsily, knocking over everything in that miserable little shack.

And that's how Inma and Puro created Maceta.

1976

Horton smokes a cigar, examining a hole in the otherwise perfect, healthy grass of his golf course.

"Looks like we have moles, Molina," he says, walking over to his golf cart. Molina comes over and inspects the hole.

"So I see."

Horton takes a pair of binoculars from the golf cart and uses them to scan the golf course.

"That's what it looks like," says Horton.

Molina laughs. Horton laughs too.

"I'd say a mole of that size . . ." says Horton, hanging the binoculars around his neck. "It must be a real monster."

"My dear Captain, don't you think it's possible that . . . ?" says Molina, making a gesture with his hands to demonstrate something coming up out of the ground. "I don't know . . . All that pressure, or, all that . . ."

Horton takes the cigar from his mouth and interrupts him.

"First, Molina, cut all that 'Captain' crap," says Horton, walking back to his golf cart, where he deposits the binoculars and removes a golf club. "You're driving me crazy with that shit. Second . . . what the hell are you talking about? This course is well constructed, it wasn't made by a Dominican. Nothing like what you're suggesting has ever happened in any of the places I researched before getting involved in this. So shut your fucking mouth."

Horton stabs the tee into the ground and places the ball on top of it.

"Some son of a bitch bent on damaging my golf course is doing this."

Horton hits the ball.

"So I want you and your people, your police, your thugs or whoever, to catch him and cut off his balls!"

Molina gets his ball ready.

"There are holes just like this one all over the course," Horton continues. "The groundskeepers can't keep up. Every time they fill one in, another appears somewhere else."

Molina hits his ball.

"That's very strange," says Molina, watching his ball sail away through the air.

"You think? . . . I've asked around. No one's seen anything."

"Of course not. No one sees anything around here."

"You people never change. I don't know what the fuck I was thinking when I decided to stay here."

"Man . . . If I had a dollar for every time I've heard you say that . . ."

Horton laughs.

"Go to hell, Molina. What I want to know is what you're going to do about it."

"Look."

Molina points to an approaching golf cart.

"That's what I'm going to do."

The golf cart pulls up alongside them. Mingo's driving. Sitting next to him is a white man with the face of a lunatic.

Some people might wonder what I mean when I say that this man had the face of a lunatic.

Let's just say that, if the head is a radio, this man's was tuned to a station that no one else on earth receives.

Or he wasn't tuned to any station at all, and the only thing he received was static.

Mingo and the man with the face of a lunatic get out of the golf cart and come to stand next to Molina.

"Horton, this is Private Benzo."

Benzo snaps to attention with a military salute and then smiles at Horton with gums as naked as a newborn baby's. Horton takes Molina aside.

"Molina . . ." says Horton, exhaling a mouthful of smoke. "You're fucking with me, right?"

"Nooo, Captain. Tell me, do you want the problem solved or not?"

"Of course I want it solved! But, this guy . . ."

"Exactly. This guy is perfect for the job. Benzo's got nothing in that head of his, he doesn't think about anything. He's a good hunting dog: he'll trap whoever's responsible for this and then he'll chop him up into pieces so tiny they'll all fit into one of the holes he made. Believe me."

Horton thinks about it.

"I don't know . . ."

"And," says Molina, smiling, "you don't have to pay him anything. You just give him some table scraps and he'll be your loyal dog for all eternity."

Molina winks at Horton. Horton smiles.

"Where the hell do you find these people?"

"Here and there . . ."

"Well, all right then."

"All you need to do is let him roam around the course. He'll pick up this mole's scent in no time. A matter of days."

"Okay, but I wouldn't want any of the club members to come across a toothless assassin out there."

Molina considers this.

"Good point, yes," he says, surveying his surroundings. "Well, let's have him patrol the fence then. Whoever's doing this is getting in over the fence."

"Yeah . . ."

"Let's see," says Molina. "Mingo, let him loose at the fence!"

Mingo and Benzo get back in the cart and drive off.

"Well, one less problem," decides Horton.

"One less problem," agrees Molina.

They walk to the golf cart. Horton turns hesitant. He stops.

"I was just thinking," he says. "How's it been going . . . getting your hands on . . . that thing we talked about the other day?"

"Eeeh . . . we found it already, we're just exerting a little pressure. I expect you should have it in hand by the end of the week."

Horton can scarcely believe it. He's bursting with joy.

"That's great news, Molina!"

"Yes, it is."

"Very good news!"

And, laughing and slapping each other on the back, each reveling in the satisfaction of goals accomplished and soon to be accomplished, these two captains of industry get into the golf cart and drive away.

Maceta, who—as we have seen—barely registers the bitternesses, difficulties, miseries, setbacks, abuses, blows and the generally deplorable panoramas that surround him, much less allows these things to put a dent in his mood and spirit of adventure, sees something that morning when he walks into the schoolyard that manages—finally!—to provoke a feeling that destroys the perpetual and miraculous equilibrium of his disposition.

His stomach hurts, but it doesn't hurt. An anthill swarms all over his body, just beneath the skin, but not exactly. Something presses against his eyes from behind, pushing them . . . or pulling them, he isn't sure. A bomb made of ice and fire that both burns and freezes his ears explodes inside his head.

Lucía, on her usual bench, is talking to another boy.

The situation is very confusing to Maceta, whose experience with jealousy is nonexistent.

He walks toward his friend. What else can he do? When Lucía sees him coming, she grabs the other boy by the hand and walks away. Maceta feels an inexplicable desire to go back home, get into bed and pull the sheet up over his head.

Inside the classroom, Lucía acts the same way. She deliberately ignores Maceta when he tries to get her attention by showing her his notebook. She turns her back to him when he shows her a drawing he's just made. She tattles to Mr. Reyna when Maceta dares to get up from his desk to give her the chocolate Merendina Vitalidad that Melisa slipped into his backpack.

During recess, Maceta spies on Lucía and is besieged by a different emotion than the jealousy with which he'd started the day. He doesn't know the name for this emotion either, but it's a pretty sure bet that we're talking about the crushing and devastating feeling of humiliation.

Crouching behind a bush scarcely big enough to hide him, he watches Lucía share her snack with the new boy and laugh at everything he says.

When he can't stand it a moment longer, he leaves his hiding place and goes to sit on their usual bench. He's not even hungry.

And then Lucía arrives.

She stands in front of him, tosses him a book and glares, her arms crossed.

"There's your stupid book," she says. "You're welcome."

Maceta picks up the book: *Gaelic Mythology and Folklore*, the very one. The book that showed him the truth about the rainbows.

Maceta forgets his prior sadness and returns to his familiar state
of joy and gratitude.

"Lucía! So, did you see how . . . ?"

"What you are is an idiot . . . a stupid little idiot. Retarded.
Un mongolo."

What can I tell you? We can't really blame her.

"Eh?" says Maceta, sounding precisely as if he were confirming the girl's diagnosis.

"And you're the worst friend I've ever had in my entire life,"
says Lucía, and she starts to cry. Maceta is worried now and, of
course, he doesn't understand anything.

"But . . ."

"Everyone talks about you . . ." Lucía says between sobs. "Maceta
here and Maceta there. Maceta this and Maceta that. Maceta to the
right and Maceta to the left. And me? I'm fine, thanks. Where have
you been? You don't tell me anything anymore!"

Maceta doesn't know how to respond.

"I didn't even want that stupid book! I bought it for you,
stupid."

Lucía falls briefly silent, considering what she's just said.

"That's not true. I didn't get it for you. It's mine!" she says, then
snatches the book from Maceta and takes off like a shot.

"Lucía!"

Maceta runs after her, clearing a path through the children
in the schoolyard. He doesn't catch her. After searching for her
for a long while, he finds her in an empty hallway. Lucía turns
her back to him.

"I'm sorry."

Lucía doesn't move. Maceta doesn't know what else to do or say.

"Where's my treasure?" Lucía asks.

"Eh?" says Maceta, again confirming Lucía's earlier assessment. She turns and faces him.

"Are you deaf? Where's my treasure? You've found treasures for everyone else, everyone except me!"

"I didn't know . . . I never know what I'm going to find."

"Liar!"

"No, Lucía! It's true!"

Lucía loses it.

"Papá says we're going to be poor soon."

Lucía thinks carefully about what she'll say next . . . and she says it.

"As poor and miserable as you."

The concept of poverty, in the way that Lucía understands it, is foreign to Maceta, and her barb doesn't manage to wound him with the severity she'd intended.

"We're going to lose our business . . . and the house and all the furniture."

Maceta is saddened by the news.

"I'm very sorry, Lucía."

"You're very sorry? What do you know about having a business, or a house . . . or furniture? I know perfectly well where you live."

This second arrow misses its target as well.

"I know you know . . . Of course you know."

"I don't need anything from you. Nothing you could give me can help us."

"People like the things I find for them. Maybe I can find something you can use. I have everything written down in my notebook."

"You're an idiot and a sucker. You think any old piece of garbage you find out there is good for something, but it's not good for anything. It's just garbage. It doesn't matter what you write down in your ridiculous little notebook. It's still just garbage. Garbage is garbage. It's no good for anything anymore, it's what people don't want and throw in the trash, it's everything that's ugly and stinks and filthy and makes you sick. You'll never find a real treasure. You don't even know what a real treasure is because you've never seen one . . . and you never will. Here . . ."

Lucía slams the book into Maceta's chest and pushes it against him.

"I don't want it anymore, because you touched it," she says.

Lucía walks away, crying. Maceta holds the book in his hands and what he says next disabuses Lucía of her notion of Maceta's supposed mental deficiency.

"I know."

Lucía stops. She turns around. Maceta has tears in his eyes, but he's not crying.

"I know how things are . . . how they really are. But . . . seeing them how . . . how they aren't is better. It's like telling a story. If I couldn't listen to that other story that things tell me, or that I tell myself . . . if things didn't speak to me . . . if they were nothing more than what they are, if I could only see them as they really are . . . the way you see them . . . what do I have? What do I have left?"

The tragedy is that these are not simply rhetorical questions. Maceta waits for Lucía to respond, his face contorted in an expression of utter helplessness. Lucía is silent. After a moment, she opens her mouth as if to say something that's stuck in her throat, then turns on her heel and runs away.

Inma, dressed in her maid's uniform, sweeps the floor of the Hortons' elegant living room.

She cleans the toilet in the enormous, luxurious bathroom. She takes out the trash. She makes the king-size bed. She irons a mountain of clothes in the service area. Kitchen.

The same as every day, except for one small difference: Inma has a black eye.

A punch from Raúl. And that's the one you can see. Beneath her clothes are the marks of other very fresh bruises.

"Inmaculada," Mrs. Horton addresses her without coming into the kitchen. Inma dries her hands on her apron and goes to stand before Mrs. Horton, who is digging around in her purse and doesn't look at her.

"Yes, ma'am."

"I'm going out in a min . . . ," Mrs. Horton starts to say, but she doesn't finish, surprised by the welt on Inma's face.

"Oh! My God!"

"It's nothing, ma'am," says Inma, touched and frankly moved by this unprecedented display of solidarity and concern.

It's never a good idea to get ahead of yourself.

"Tell me!" Mrs. Horton demands. "What did you do this time?"

Inma abruptly changes her expression, swallows hard and notices that her eye is twitching. Mrs. Horton looks away from her and goes back to rooting about in her purse.

"The truth is I'll just never understand you people . . ."

You people? Inma thinks. *You people?*

Mrs. Horton finally finds her wallet and opens it.

"Well, look . . . I need to go out and I won't be back until after you leave."

Mrs. Horton takes out a pair of bills and a few coins and hands them to Inma.

"Here are your wages."

Inma closes her fist around the money. Mrs. Horton closes her wallet and puts it back in her purse.

"I subtracted the blouse you damaged last week and the jar of mayonnaise you broke the other day. Aside from that, it should all be there. Count it if you want."

She starts to leave, but then she remembers something else.

"Oh, and please clean up the mess the dogs left on the lawn before you go."

"Yes, ma'am."

Addicts call it a "moment of clarity."

Mrs. Horton leaves and Inma goes back to the kitchen, moving among the bubbling pots. She still holds the money crushed in one hand as she stirs the soup with the other. At a certain point, she finds she needs to use her other hand and that's when she realizes she's still holding the money. She looks at it with contempt and disgust, as though it were a dead animal. Finally, she puts it in her pocket and continues working.

But then her body begins to convulse involuntarily. Inma is the first to be surprised. But it's not epilepsy or a heart attack. She's simply sobbing.

Uncontrollably.

The knowledge that she's sobbing only makes her angrier, and she begins to wail. Finding herself blubbering like a baby, with hiccups and snot, like a total pendeja, fills her with rage and she slams the spoon she'd been using down on the stove, splattering soup all over the place.

She dries her tears with the back of her hand, yanks off her apron, throws it on the floor and walks out of the kitchen.

Inma puts on her rubber gloves and goes outside. She walks around the yard, ignoring the ferocious rottweilers who are throwing themselves against the chain-link fence of the dog run, and starts collecting dog shit in a tin can.

When she has enough, Inma goes into the master bedroom, strips the king-size bed, and smears the mattress with poop from top to bottom. She takes what's left in the can into Mrs. Horton's closet and deposits it in her shoes. When the can is empty, she wipes it out with one of Mrs. Horton's favorite dresses.

Sow the wind, reap the whirlwind. If the tiniest hint of body odor is enough to set her off, just imagine what happened when Mrs. Horton returned home.

With her purse over her shoulder and a lightweight blouse over her maid's uniform, Inma leaves the Horton mansion and is heading toward the street just as the captain parks his Mercedes-Benz and gets out.

"Where the hell do you think you're going?" he sneers. "You still have a couple of hours of work left."

"Go to hell, you goddamned Yankee!" Inma shouts without looking at him.

Mamagüela's an old-school prieta.

Horton can't believe it.

"What did you say?"

Inma, who's already a fair distance away, turns around and walks over to Horton, who backs up, intimidated. She jabs her index finger into his chest and looks him straight in the eye:

"I said: Go to fucking hell, you goddamned Yankee!"

Inma looks at him a moment longer. Horton is petrified. Inma turns away from him and walks off, leaving him squashed up against the side of his car.

"You can all go straight to hell!" Inma reiterates as she walks away.

Horton waits until she's at the front gate.

"Eeeh . . . well, you go to hell too, you ungrateful chopa!" he shouts. "I looked out for you, bitch. If it weren't for me? Tell me!"

Horton violently slams his car door.

"Fucking people . . ." he says between gritted teeth and goes inside his house.

Maceta is sad. Dejected, he walks along the path that borders the golf course. He's not in the mood for rainbows . . . but some habits are hard to break. He sits with his shovel on his usual tree trunk to wait for the sprinklers.

The sprinklers come on and the rainbow appears, but Maceta doesn't move. Only after a good long while, and grudgingly, like someone fulfilling an obligation, does he toss the shovel over and hop the fence.

Pulling out a final fistful of earth, Maceta peers into the hole he's just dug. He reaches his hand in and pulls out a strange, red artifact with two eyepieces and a lever on its right-hand side. It looks like a pair of binoculars.

His examination of the treasure is interrupted when Private Benzo's pale hand grabs him by the hair and lifts him into the air. Maceta's feet dangle, seeking the ground, and he is horrified to see before him the unhinged recruit giving him a toothless smile, his bug eyes threatening to jump out of their sockets.

Maceta screams.

With inexplicable force, Benzo shakes him several times and tosses him far away from where he's standing. Maceta falls face-first in a sand trap. He sits up shakily and turns around; Benzo smiles again, takes out an enormous butcher's knife, and walks toward him. Maceta gets to his feet and runs away in terror.

Running for all he's worth, Maceta trips, gets back up, keeps running, while Benzo appears to advance as if floating through the air, quick as a gazelle, immune to exhaustion. Maceta can barely stay on his feet: fatigue and terror overcome him. Benzo reaches him at last when Maceta collapses, spent, on the grass.

Maceta lies face up, awaiting the inevitable, and for a brief moment, he notes that it's a lovely day with a cloudless sky. But this very blue sky is obscured now by Benzo's huge head as the man kneels over Maceta, brandishing the knife aloft, ready to kill him.

The only thing Maceta can think to do is close his eyes and shield himself with the treasure he's just unearthed, thrusting it up into Benzo's face.

Nothing happens.

The knife doesn't go through him, his blood doesn't spill out.

Another minute and still nothing happens.

Maceta dares to open his eyes and he discovers Benzo spellbound, looking through the eyepieces of the View-Master Maceta is holding before his eyes.

The killer drops the knife and takes the contraption in his hands.

What Benzo sees in the View-Master: a photograph of the Statue of Liberty.

Maceta moves cautiously out from under Benzo, but he doesn't run away. Instead, he studies the toy and then works the lever to change the image.

Benzo makes the guttural noise of an animal consumed with pleasure. He's understood how the gadget works and now he's operating it by himself. Every time the image changes he laughs and delights like a child. Maceta gives him a friendly pat on the shoulder and walks away, never taking his eyes off him.

His flight has taken him to the other side of the golf course, back to the shack in the scrub thicket where, days earlier, the rainbow had led him. The place that Loco Abril had half-heartedly defended.

Maceta sighs and jumps the fence.

He makes his way through the undergrowth until he comes to the derelict's shack. He looks around, making sure he's alone, and goes inside.

The inside of the shack is astonishing. Faint sunlight filters through a skylight, illuminating a room furnished with items obviously collected from garbage dumps. Maceta, intrigued, looks around until he sees a switch affixed precariously to the wall. He flips the switch. A lamp comes on, illuminating the entire space. Now Maceta can see a staircase cut into the stone floor, leading down to some other place.

Maceta descends, amazed. He comes to a landing that leads to more stairs going yet farther down, disappearing into the darkness. After descending for a long time, Maceta reaches the final step, and in the now faint light from above, he sees another switch. Maceta flips it. And then there is light.

Maceta finds himself in a vast underground library. The walls, with shelves carved out of the limestone, are filled with books from floor to ceiling. There is a desk and a couch next to another little table. Everything is old and mismatched, but clean and orderly. There is not a single speck of dust.

On one wall are two Kalashnikovs, which Maceta strokes with curiosity. The wall across from the desk is covered with old photographs. It's a motley, overcrowded collage. Most of the photos are in black and white. The theme, quite evidently, is the Civil War of '65: groups of armed combatants, both men and women; US soldiers aiming their weapons; battles, tanks, ships, barricades, bodies.

The photos that no historian has ever asked us to see as they're writing their books every bit as full of holes as Captain Horton's golf course.

Maceta feels especially drawn to the photos of a young mulato, tall and thin, wearing thick black-rimmed glasses. The man poses, standing straight as a fencepost, with other important-looking men, his expression unwaveringly serious, dignified. He poses next to Francisco Caamaño, next to Professor Juan Bosch, with soldiers, with students, with demonstrators, and individually with smiling men and women among whom Maceta thinks he recognizes Jacinto and Eneida, an extremely young Don Chago, and Lidio, the auto body mechanic, impossible to mistake for anyone else . . .

But the man in the glasses appears most frequently in the photos alongside a young man with a pencil-thin mustache, short and fat, dressed in an impeccable military uniform and with a meticulously shaved face.

Maceta takes one photo down from the wall and examines it; an image of the two men linked in an embrace, smiling.

"That's your father . . ." comes Loco Abril's gravelly voice from behind Maceta's turned back.

Maceta gives a start and falls to the ground. He's so frightened he pisses himself a little.

But he doesn't drop the photograph. The madman laughs, drops a threadbare sack to the floor, walks over to Maceta, grabs the photo and looks at it, remembering.

"The other man is me," he says. "Well . . . It was me."

Loco Abril looks at Maceta and holds the photo up next to his head.

"But I haven't really changed all that much, have I?"

The madman waits for Maceta's response, which, of course, never comes, and he starts to laugh. Suddenly, he turns serious again, looking at Maceta in astonishment. Loco Abril gives the photo back to Maceta, who looks at it now with particular interest.

"Puro Maceta," the madman declares. "The best, most charming man who was ever born."

Then he takes another photo from the wall and gives it to Maceta.

"Do you know who that is?"

The photo shows a mulato man—a three-quarters Black indio, he used to say—middle-aged, with a rifle slung across his back, smiling with broad, white teeth. His face is jovial, affable. Maceta looks at the madman without speaking.

"That's your grandfather, Pancho Carmona, your mother's father," he explains, laughing and walking away from Maceta. "The biggest crook there ever was. But, but, but . . . politically motivated."

Loco Abril sits down on the couch and puts his feet up on the coffee table.

"The Yankees killed him," says Loco Abril. "The provisional government confiscated all his assets. They left his family out in the street."

Loco Abril furiously scratches his beard, discharging a poorly contained, misguided, old, festering and in the end, irrelevant, rage. Maceta, still holding the two photos, looks at him, trying to puzzle things out.

"You and my father were friends?"

Loco Abril looks at Maceta, tilting his head, scrunching up his eyes.

"Inmaculada has done her job well," he says. "There's no need to go rummaging around in the past. What for? It's better this way."

The madman opens his eyes wide in alarm and looks at Maceta as though he's just arrived.

"What are you doing here? How did you get here?"

There's no answer. Little by little, Loco Abril calms down.

"Your father was a very intelligent man," he says after a while, "the most brilliant of us all. And what a smooth talker! He could sell you a bag of sand in the desert . . . Yes he could. Not much of a fighter. Nearsighted. Asthmatic . . . Useless in battle. That's the truth . . . But heaven help the man who thought to tell him so!"

Loco Abril smooths his beard with his hand. Maceta sits down at the desk.

"Everyone loved him ... everyone," he says, cracking his knuckles. "And immediately: you met him, you heard him speak, and you already loved him ... I don't know ... I don't know what it was about him. Some people are just born with it."

Loco Abril thinks quietly for a few brief moments and then he points to a large photo up toward the top of the collage.

"But that son of a bitch up there?"

Maceta looks up. And he sees the image of a young Molina posing with a rifle, his right foot resting on the body of a dead US soldier.

"He was juuuust the opposite."

Maceta keeps looking at the photo. The madman is lost in his memories.

"It didn't matter what he did or what he said ... no one ever liked him. That asshole couldn't win over a starving dog, even if he came bearing a salami. There was something about him that made everyone hate him ... He was born with it, just like your father was born with the other thing."

Loco Abril looks up; something has just occurred to him.

"Which is very strange," he says. "Ironic and strange because ... well."

Loco Abril scratches his thighs with both hands and abandons the thought.

"But ... you father is dead and that scumbag is alive and kicking, so ... what's the lesson?" he says and then mutters to himself: "What's the lesson? What's the lesson? What's the lesson? What's the ... ?"

Loco Abril smiles, looks mischievously at Maceta.

"Do you want to know the last thing your father made before he died?"

Maceta nods.

"You."

Loco Abril bursts out in a guffaw. Motionless, Maceta watches him laugh.

"Really, it was you."

The madman's laughter subsides. Maceta doesn't understand a thing. The madman turns serious, gives Maceta a sad, melancholy look. His body begins rocking slowly, rhythmically in his seat, as if in time to a song only he can hear.

"Yes . . . yes. He was my friend, your father was my friend . . . My best friend in the whole world."

Loco Abril goes quiet and that silence extends like a geological age.

"And it was my fault that they killed him," he says at last.

Maceta looks at him, stunned.

"It was me. It was my fault that they killed him, my fault that they killed him, my fault that they killed him, my fault that they killed him, my fault that they kil . . ."

Loco Abril tries hard to stop himself from talking. He covers his mouth with both hands. He slaps himself. He stops slapping himself. Suddenly he kneels in front of the coffee table.

"How did I kill him?" he says, looking at Maceta. "I'm glad you asked."

He pushes the table and lifts a scrap of carpet to reveal an old, rusted metal box built into the floor and secured with an enormous padlock. He searches beneath his ragged shirt—and his dirty beard—and pulls out a key hanging from a chain about his neck.

"I made some very, very bad people . . ." he says, making spasmodic, agitated movements that make it difficult for him to get the key into the lock.

". . . believe . . ."

Loco Abril puts the key in the lock.

". . . that your father . . ."

Loco Abril opens the box.

". . . had this."

Inside, neatly arranged, are three solid-gold ingots.

I've always heard it said that the defining characteristic of madness is doing the same thing over and over and expecting a different result each time. And it's always seemed to me that this statement is extremely limited. Especially in the case of Loco Abril and others like him, people who are unquestionably crazy, their sanity irretrievably lost.

I would add that any madman worthy of the name is incapable of recognizing contexts, of adjusting to situations, of recognizing the subtleties inherent to the immensity of human diversity. A madman talks to everyone in exactly the same way, whether they're a man, a woman, rich, poor, elderly or a child. That's also why they say you have to be careful with madmen, drunks and children, because they always tell the truth without anticipating the consequences.

The fools in classical tragedies are madmen, drunks or children, and even the kings listen carefully to their impertinences without retaliating.

An adult who behaves like a child is certainly crazy, and a drunk is a child for as long as his drunkenness lasts. A child is a child and can't help being so, and that's why it isn't unsettling that they act like children. What would be unsettling is a child who acts like an adult, and in this respect Maceta gets very high marks, no matter how innocent and naive he might seem to us.

And so, Loco Abril has no qualms about unloading the complicated story of his betrayal as if he were speaking to an equal, and Maceta doesn't find it at all odd that the madman considers it appropriate to tell him these things. So, though he may be incapable of understanding certain details, he listens with careful attention to how Loco Abril, before he was crazy, was named Oviedo and was sleeping with Major McCollum.

He was sleeping with McCollum? Does that mean they shared a house, like he did with his family? That they were poor and had only one bed? That they took naps together, like he and his Aunt Melisa did on Saturday afternoons?

The rest is even more enigmatic, but profoundly interesting.

Oviedo was recruited early on. When McCollum laid out the proposal to him he didn't think twice. Here's my chance to shine, out from under Puro's shadow and Molina's obvious depravity. Here's my chance to really do something, to have a real adventure, to put my life on the line, to be a true hero.

Oviedo reported the meeting to high command and received orders to accept. Not even Puro knew about it, much less Molina. Sarah McCollum was his sole and exclusive point of contact.

Sarah ...

Loco Abril stumbles over her name, his vocal cords get jammed, the name strangles him, chokes him.

Maceta notices but he's unable to interpret the distress, the suffering that the name causes him.

But I can, my daughters, I can.

In the end, Oviedo's reasons for becoming a double agent are not the ones he confessed to Maceta. A yearning for the limelight, revenge against Puro, vengeance against Molina ...

No.

Oviedo was a Caribbean man through and through and he shared the same cardinal weakness with every other full-blooded Caribbean man: the white woman.

Don't make that face. Better to learn it the easy way now than learn it the hard way later. That prince who swears he loves and adores you, which isn't even necessarily a lie, will kick you to the curb for the first blonde who smiles at him. And she doesn't even have to be pretty.

As for Major McCollum, Oviedo was doubly damned, because McCollum was an Irish Amazon who looked like a pinup straight out of a magazine.

God only knows how they met and under what circumstances. Probably in a bar in the Security Zone. Or maybe in a piano bar in some beachfront hotel. Oviedo always loved the hustle and bustle of the tourist spots. He picked up a few tourists here and there. And whenever delegations from the Socialist International came to meet with Peña Gómez or with Juan Bosch, Oviedo would take it upon himself to entertain the females, and not just the single ones.

In McCollum, Oviedo had met his match. The seas parted. No one else existed. Especially because Sarah fell in love too . . .

But let's see here . . . We're using the phrase "to fall in love" a bit loosely. According to other accounts, Sarah was not the sort of woman who fell in love. But even women who don't fall in love fall in love, and always with the person one least expects. And so it doesn't surprise me that she would have gone . . . berserk for Oviedo.

And when a woman like that goes berserk . . .

That was Oviedo's mistake, the biggest one of all: underestimating the feelings he had aroused in Major McCollum. Believing himself unworthy. Thinking he was alone in his infatuation. There's an endless supply of men and women incapable of believing themselves blessed, even in the midst of their own good fortune.

They loved each other, Oviedo told Maceta. They loved each other in secret. McCollum knew that Oviedo was passing along to the rebels any information that she let slip while in the throes of love, and sometimes she made things up, and sometimes she didn't, because she wanted them to trust Oviedo, or simply because she loved him. No one knows.

Oviedo never made things up. Everything that he told McCollum, on the one hand, and his fellow constitutionalists, on the other, was one hundred percent correct.

Oviedo was a snitch, but a snitch with moral fiber and ethical standards.

A real hero.

Oviedo knew perfectly well that McCollum was batshit crazy, that she was dangerous. He had seen his comrades-in-arms, captured thanks to his activities as an informant, enter the Security Zone as human beings and come out as hamburger meat. That's why, when the major proposed that he intercept the bribe money that the military junta had agreed to pay the invading army, he knew the moment had come to say goodbye.

At first he thought it was a trap, that his lover had decided to end their relationship with a bang. But the determination, zeal and meticulousness of her preparations began to convince him that the truth was even more terrible still: Sarah was serious. Sarah wanted to run away with him to someplace where no one would ever find them, escape to the ends of the earth if necessary. Sarah wanted to get married, have a family. Sarah, Major McCollum, the intelligence agent who had made the most sadistic of the dictatorship's Military Intelligence Service henchmen tremble, wanted to play house, but for real.

How to disappoint a woman like McCollum? How to reject her, to spurn her, to dump her?

Oviedo understood then that he had only one option: he had to shoot her.

The operation was a ruse. The junta had already made the payment a month earlier. Those ingots were hidden deep inside the armored belly of the USS *Boxer*. No one had suspected a thing.

McCollum suggested that they leak the news to the constitutionalists, not as a done deal, but as a deal to be done. The objective: identify the mole who had infiltrated the marines' high command. The mole was McCollum herself, obviously, but only Oviedo knew that. The major needed an excuse and valid credentials to enter and leave the vault of the USS *Boxer*.

Informed of the official plan, Horton sprays three heavy lead ingots with gold spray paint and stamps them with the Central Bank of the Dominican Republic watermark.

Later, and at great risk to her hide, McCollum enters the vault and swaps the lead ingots for three real ones.

No one will find out about it until much later, when the warship drops anchor at the Roosevelt Roads naval station, in Puerto Rico.

By that time, thinks McCollum, she and Oviedo will be far, far away.

It was a clandestine operation and it would take place at Port Sans Souci.

That night, two Dominican soldiers—in reality, two civilians disguised by McCollum to dramatize the scene—head down one of the side streets adjacent to the pier. They are carrying a heavy suitcase—*the* suitcase.

Major McCollum and a private wait for them beneath a streetlamp.

The Dominican soldiers hold the suitcase out to the North Americans.

Oviedo and Elsa come out of their hiding places and unceremoniously kill the Dominican soldiers. Elsa shoots and kills the private with McCollum, but when she's about to kill the major, she is shot in the back.

Oviedo.

Sarah . . .

It hurts to say her name.

After killing Elsa, who had been Puro's close friend, Oviedo embraces McCollum, and she embraces him back, tightly and passionately.

There would be time for that later. Now it was time to handle matters and get out of there.

Oviedo opens the suitcase, takes out the ingots and places them in a steel case. He passes the case to the major.

Oviedo knows that Molina is working for Horton, and that the two of them will soon take it upon themselves to catch the commando unit red-handed. Oviedo puts a photo of Molina in Elsa's shirt pocket—a photo of the traitor, in case the commandos make it out of the ambush—with a date and an address written on the back: when and where Puro and his cronies will meet again.

Oviedo stands up.

McCollum, steel case in hand, looks at him adoringly.

Oviedo shoots her in the face.

At daybreak, carrying the steel case and the empty suitcase—the one the marines would recognize in Puro's hands—Oviedo moves deep into the bush. He holds on to the suitcase, but he buries the steel case with the ingots in a deep hole hidden in the tangled thicket where he would eventually build his hideout.

Did he know then that this would be his home for the rest of his life?

I think he did.

Everyone tells the story in the way that suits them best and interprets their decisions so that they appear in the best possible light.

Who knows? Maybe I'm doing the exact same thing.

No one wants to be the bad guy in the movie, especially the bad guy in the movie.

Oviedo does not run, he does not disappear, he does not cross the border into Haiti, he does not take a small plane to Cuba, though it would have been easy to do so.

No.

Oviedo takes the empty suitcase that the imposter soldiers provided him and, on the day of the meeting, he climbs to the rooftop of a building on Padre Billini and spies on Puro making his rounds. He looks like an American movie hero, like Che Guevara, but darker skinned, a touch shorter, a touch fatter, a touch more serious, but just a touch. Dressed in army fatigues like Fidel Castro's guerrillas, like Fidel Castro himself, and although his uniform wasn't new, it was well cared for, clean, it smelled like detergent.

On that day, exactly fifty-two years ago, when Loco Abril was known by a regular first name, a regular last name, and held the rank of commander.

Loco Abril's eyes, flooded with tears, can scarcely focus on Maceta, who is listening, enraptured.

"I knew that soon all hell would break loose. I could have simply left . . . but I couldn't. Puro didn't know what he would be receiving, so it didn't matter what I gave him."

Loco Abril remembers that afternoon, remembers Puro greeting and being greeted; remembers Inma dying of love for him and Puro dying of love for her.

"But I took the trouble of putting something in there that would have meaning only for him . . . One final joke between friends."

Loco Abril remembers Oviedo coming down the alleyway, remembers Puro smoking patiently, leaning with one foot against a peeling wall, next to a solid metal door.

He remembers their embrace.

Judas also kissed Jesus on the night he sold him for thirty silver pieces.

"I could have left . . ." says Oviedo, kneeling before the ingots, "but some of us only rarely have the opportunity to shine . . ."

Joining Loco Abril on the ground, Maceta kneels and studies the gold ingots. The madman's eyes are red and yellow . . . and blue and green and orange and indigo, like the oily puddles on the pavement after a downpour.

"Everyone loved your father. And everyone hated Molina. They both had that certain something . . . Me, on the other hand, everyone ignored me. That was my thing, to be invisible. A perfect snitch. Everything I did . . . I did it so I could shine, to stand out, to be noticed, to be needed, to be respected, to be hated . . . or to be loved . . . To *be*."

No. No.

Oviedo did not head for safety and returned instead to the lion's den, but it wasn't for any of these reasons, no matter how much he wanted to believe them. Oviedo returned to receive the punishment he deserved. Or to heroically save Puro from the shootout.

Or to die with him.

Judas, who had more sense, chose to hang himself. There are some things you just can't leave up to chance.

Loco Abril looks at Maceta and Maceta discovers that, there before him, Oviedo has begun to regain some lost ground.

Maceta lowers his gaze. Loco Abril locks the box and hangs the key around Maceta's neck. Maceta strokes it and tucks it beneath his shirt.

"The gold is yours. But you have to come back for it when you can protect it from those who will want to take it from you. Which is about half of the human race."

They stand up together. Maceta walks toward the stairs, but he pauses before ascending. He has one last question.

"What will you do now?"

Oviedo smiles at him.

"I have been paying off what I owe every day for the past eleven years," he says. "Now it's time to square the remaining balance."

When he is alone once more, Oviedo opens another box, this one even more carefully hidden than the box with the treasure in it, and takes out a military uniform. He finds a pair of scissors, soap, a razor.

We're in the home stretch! Our story is nearly at its end. I've sweat blood and tears going backward and forward and forward and backward, and there's nothing worse than trying to tell something to a pair of stubborn, self-important, overgrown little girls like the two of you. I ought to send you to spend a few days in the neighborhood where my story takes place just to see if you can hack it, or enroll you for a semester in Maceta's school, which still exists, and with that apple-polisher Mr. Reyna as the principal, no less.

Kick your butts right out of your comfy little lives. Expose you to problems that are actually worth their weight in tears and see if that stops you from spilling them every time you crack the screen on your iPhone and I refuse to pay to have it repaired. Throw you right into the fire and see if you'll finally come to appreciate what you have and how much it's cost us to get it, because the trip from the bottom to the top is brutal and it's hard work and it takes two or more generations to complete . . . but the trip from the top to the bottom is a cinch, and you can make it there nonstop in one generation.

Since I can't put this plan into action because your indulgent father would object, I am hoping that my story will allow you to learn from the experiences of others, the old proverb notwithstanding.

I expect you're both pleased, since you each got exactly what you wanted out of the story. I'm sorry to tell you, however, that I'm about to take the plunge and reveal a couple of things that you won't want to hear, but that you need to hear.

They say that to learn to cross a river you have to bang your head against the river bottom.

This is the river bottom.

Evelio was always insubstantial, timid, a crybaby, a coward; not like his father, Gregorio, a man of action, garrulous, friendly, decisive. Some people felt that Don Gregorio shouldn't have died so young and everyone felt that, if he had to die, he shouldn't have died without leaving a will. His only son, Evelio, inherited businesses he didn't know how to run, a fortune he was unable to retain, and a reputation he couldn't uphold.

Standing in the hallway between the kitchen and the living room, Evelio Méndez watches his three children playing. His is a modest home, decent, with all the modern comforts: washer, dryer, refrigerator, radio, color TV.

Telephone.

Evelio walks over to a side table on which sits a black rotary phone.

Evelio dials a number.

"Yes, hello," he says into the phone. "Connect me to Mr. Molina please. Tell him it's Evelio. Thank you . . ."

Evelio's children laugh. One of them whines a complaint. Another placates him.

"Good afternoon to you too," Evelio says into the telephone and sighs. "Yes, yes . . . in fact . . . in fact, I've thought it over very carefully . . . Of course . . . There's no problem at all . . . If you'd like, you can come by right now and we can finalize our . . ."

Evelio was going to say "business," but his tongue refuses to form the word.

"Excellent," Evelio says as he hangs up the phone and closes his eyes.

"Sweetheart . . . ?" Evelio calls out to the children. Of the three, only one responds to this endearment. She breaks away from her younger siblings and comes over to Evelio.

"Yes, Daddy?" says Lucía.

"Go get changed, fix yourself up nice and pretty for me. We're going out for a spin."

Molina hangs up the phone, picks it up again and dials a number.

"Horton? . . . Congratulations! . . . What did I tell you? . . . No, no, I'll see you in half an hour . . . At the usual hole . . . Nah, I need to get back early. The Chinese are coming tonight, but thanks for the invitation . . . All of the Chinese. It's a done deal, my brother . . . Of course. See you soon."

Molina hangs up the phone, happy as the worm that he is.

But Mingo comes into the office and stops in front of Molina. Molina looks at him.

"Boss . . ."

"What is it, Mingo?"

"We have a little problem. There's not a single woman in the Molina Sports Bar & Casino."

"Not a single one?" asks Molina, alarmed.

"Not a single one," replies Mingo.

Not a single one. They'd all looked at themselves in Clarisa and Melisa's *mirror mirror* and realized, unexpectedly and simultaneously, that they didn't want to go back there, that they wouldn't go back there and allow themselves to be felt up by fat drunks with bad breath for anything in the world.

"Well . . ." Mingo reconsiders. "Chachi's over there."

Mingo points to a skeletal, ugly woman who greets them with an undeniably lewd gesture. Molina closes his eyes and breathes deeply.

"Chachi doesn't even work here, Mingo."

"Sorry, boss."

"How many times do I have to tell you not to let her in here?"

"I know, boss . . . but I thought that under the circum- stances . . ."

Molina sucks his upper lip in frustration.

"I don't have time for this right now! Find them! Find all of them! And bring them back here before it gets dark!" Molina orders and stomps off.

"Yes, boss."

"And get Chachi out of here!" he shouts before disappearing into the tunnel that connects to his office.

Inma gets off the bus, a very unfriendly look on her face. She's furious, she's mad as hell. She's breathing fire. People who know her step to the side. People who don't know her do too. This wouldn't be known until much later, but grass never again grew where Inma walked that day.

Inma passes by a bar from which comes, just at that moment, a loud guffaw. She stops dead. She knows that laugh. Inma changes direction and heads for the establishment.

There, Raúl is drinking a beer and chatting in a very intimate way with a beautiful, voluptuous woman. They're sitting at the bar alongside other men smoking, drinking, shooting the breeze. Inma sees it all from the street and moves stealthily toward them.

"That's not true . . ." Raúl is saying, playful, his face very near the woman's face.

"Oh, yes . . ." responds the woman, provocatively.

"No."

"Yes."

Inma is almost to the door, but the couple is so absorbed in their flirtation that they don't see her coming.

"I want to see it," says Raúl.

"And I want to show it to you . . ." says the woman.

What happens next has been preserved for posterity in the oral mythology of the neighborhood and is known, even today, as "the time Inma beat Raúl bald."

Inma walks into the place and the first thing she does is grab Raúl's beer bottle and smash it over his skull.

The woman who'd been fooling around with him screams like a banshee and runs out of the bar.

The rest of the patrons stop drinking, stop smoking and stop chatting in order to concentrate on what Inma does next, which is to grab Raúl by the hair and drag him into the street.

Raúl, needless to say, is not well-loved by the community, and most everyone always wondered what Inma saw in him or what he did to her that she would put up with so much shit. I say this because, from this moment forward, everything that happens will happen in the middle of a deafening uproar, amid a riot of humans who surround them, moving with them en masse up the street like an ever-changing and unstable kaleidoscope. Everyone cheers Inma on, encouraging her to kick her sorry, good-for-nothing, piece of shit, freeloading boyfriend's ass.

Inma goes out into the street with Raúl, dragging him by the hair. Raúl is bleeding profusely from the wound to his head. He's dizzy and disoriented. When Inma lets go of his hair, Raúl falls flat on his back and lies on the ground, his legs splayed. Inma, not missing a beat, stomps on his testicles with the heel of her shoe, bearing down with her full weight.

The crowd goes wild.

Inma proceeds to unbuckle Raúl's belt and pull it from his pants. She folds it in two and begins to whip the man with such obvious passion and pleasure that the crowd would have been fully satisfied if she'd left it at that.

But Inma isn't anywhere near satisfied.

Lashes rain down on every part of Raúl's body: his back, his chest, his face . . . He tries to get away and comes up against a pair of garbage cans. Inma drops the belt and grabs one of the can's lids and slams it down on Raúl's head. The crowd applauds and cheers and counts each wallop Inma delivers with the trash can lid.

¡Uno!

¡Dos!

¡Tres!

¡Cuatro! ¡Cinco! ¡Seis!

¡Siete, coño!

Now Raúl gets ahold of a stick, a rotten branch from a sapodilla tree, manages to get to his feet, and tries to hit Inma with it. And he would have hit her, if it weren't for the fact that he's still cross-eyed from the blow to the head with the beer bottle and the kick to his nuts and the lashes with the belt and the seven wallops with the trash can lid. Not only does Inma sidestep him easily, but she also deals him a right hook to the jaw that lands him right back on the ground.

Among the onlookers cheering her on is a vendor of handmade brooms.

"Genaro!" Inma calls out to him.

The vendor anticipates her request and hands her one of his brooms. Inma, transformed now into a wrathful witch, walks over to Raúl and takes the measure of his ribs with the broom until it breaks. The people cheer and applaud.

Crawling down the street, Raúl manages to put a little distance between himself and Inma. Inma follows him, leisurely; she tosses the broom away and kicks him in the backside. Raúl falls face-first in a muddy puddle.

The crowd, meanwhile, keeps growing.

At last, Inma and Raúl pause near a gutter in which lies the bloated corpse of a stray dog that didn't look both ways before crossing the street, and which the crowd expertly avoids as it follows the couple. Raúl tries to stand, but he can't, and he continues dragging himself along like the snake in the grass he's always been.

Inma notices the dog's mortal remains and walks in that direction. The crowd, guessing at her intentions, goes wild, the volume of their jubilation rising to a fever pitch. Inma grabs the dog's rear paws, making sure she's got a firm grasp on them, and walks with the swollen cadaver towards Raúl.

What can you say about a man who gets basted in public with a dead dog?

No one ever saw Raúl in the neighborhood again.

While Inma is making mincemeat of Raúl in the outskirts of the neighborhood—out where the buses stop and the motorcycle taxis wait in the shade for their fares—Mingo and a dozen thugs are moving down Maceta's street.

They pass by Tomás and Simón, who stop shaking the eight ball in order to watch the malevolent procession of men carrying machetes, clubs and bats. They walk by Jacinto and Eneida's place, interrupting a lively game of basketball on a small, improvised court in front of the house, pushing aside the players standing in their path.

The air hums with the flock of birds that gather at that time of day to fill their gullets from Mercedes's bird feeders, and which, instinctively interpreting the depraved nature of the invaders, shit all over them. The killers flap their hands as though waving away mosquitos, and they hunch over and run as if caught in a rainstorm.

The flowers planted in old cans and pots present the killers with an explosion of colors—and scents—that blinds and befuddles them, apart from which, they have no idea what the hell that music coming from one of the houses could be, music that takes control of their bodies, putting a sway in their hips and a swing in their steps that does not correlate with the violence of their intentions. And so, confused and disoriented, they knock over the pots, stomp on the flowers, and one of them goes into Jorge Aníbal's house and smashes the record player.

Mingo and his procession of thugs arrive at their destination: Inma's house. Beneath the tamarind tree, the twins have set up a "cosmetology and beauty school." All the girls from the brothel are taking classes, standing behind volunteer clients who are explaining how they want their hair done. Mingo and his throng bust in and start wrecking things, violently grabbing the girls. Mayhem ensues.

The girls fight valiantly to defend themselves, but Mingo's thugs subdue them, smashing everything in their path. The neighborhood clusters around the ruckus, but no one dares to intervene. A short time later, a truck with a green tarp over its bed pulls up.

Mingo and his men force the girls into the truck. Several of the men get in with them, closing the tailgate. Everyone else disperses on foot.

Mingo climbs into the passenger seat and speaks to the driver.

"Step on it. These bitches have to get to work."

It is difficult, if not impossible, for the driver to respond, owing to the clean slit across his throat and the blood spurting from his mouth.

"La creta!"

Someone opens the passenger door and grabs Mingo roughly by the neck, pulling him from the truck. Mingo, sprawled on the ground, tries to stand up quickly and bumps into a man dressed in military fatigues brandishing a sharp, pointy Collins knife in each hand. Mingo backs up and his thugs surround the madman, sticks and rocks at the ready.

Oviedo cuts them down one by one, cold and precise. He dispatches them easily, there's no need to go into detail. Suffice to say that a head and a pair of ears rolled and very few fingers remained attached to the hands to which they had belonged.

But the men who had gotten into the truck with the women now climb out, and these men are armed with cane machetes.

The girls peek out, but they are too afraid to get out of the truck. A ferocious and uneven fight ensues. No one makes any noise. The only sounds are the moans of the men when they are wounded. Oviedo sustains a few slash wounds—to the chest, the left arm, the face and one calf—but, with military efficiency, he continues to dispatch his foes one by one.

Oviedo's style demonstrates a fine balance of thrusts, slices and feints. He enters his opponent's space with a feint and then immediately retreats, confusing the enemy in front of him and forcing him to block the Collins knife in his left hand, at which point Oviedo takes advantage of the opportunity to stab the adversary behind him with the Collins knife in his right hand.

His foes can do nothing but slash at him, limited as they are by the curved blades of their cane machetes. You have to prepare to make a good cut with a machete: raise the blade backwards, at any angle, and let it fall forward. There's no way to hide your intention. Whenever his foe raises an arm, Oviedo already knows that he should be ready for a blow; and when this same foe brings his arm forcefully forward, no matter which direction it comes from, the inertia forces the machete to commit to that trajectory and to that trajectory alone. Oviedo calculates where the machete blows will fall several seconds before they fall. From his perspective, his opponents are fighting in slow motion, bogged down by the momentum of the machetes, which are not weapons after all, but rather farming implements.

The Collins knife, on the other hand, allow Oviedo to lance and to stab. And you don't need to raise your arm and allow it to fall in order to stab. A good knife thrust is accomplished by pulling your arm in toward your own abdomen and driving it forward toward your rival's stomach, limb, throat or face. But pulling your arm in can also be the origin of a good slash, and Mingo's thugs don't know what to expect from Oviedo each time he folds like a cucurucho, because the movement might be followed by a stab or by a slash.

And this is how he kills them, one by one.

Just one opponent remains standing: Mingo.

And Mingo is not carrying a machete, but rather a long and very sharp lengua de mime.

Mime is the Taíno word for Drosophila, the common fruit fly.

Lengua is a mobile muscular hydrostat, singular and symmetrical, located in the mouth to assist in the processes of salivation and the swallowing of food.

Lengua de mime is a lightweight knife of variable length, ranging between that of a dagger and a foil, with a rigid blade (single or double-edged), a simple hilt and a long grip made of transparent resin covering a cylindrical handle decorated in three colors: red, white and black, in that order, from the hilt to the pommel.

Mingo's lengua de mime possessed all of these characteristics and also boasted a groove down the blade for his opponent's blood. It was a gift from the brother of a Haitian girlfriend he'd had years before when he'd had to hide out for a while in Croix Hilaire.

Killing Mingo was not going to be easy.

Oviedo and Mingo study one another for several moments. Oviedo is bleeding profusely from his multiple wounds, but his face betrays neither concern nor pain. Mingo is unscathed, but he wears a crazed, desperate expression. A half hour of well-executed feints, stabs and slashes ensues. It is a highly technical and supremely boring battle.

After half an hour, Mingo runs out of patience and starts making mistakes. There's nothing worse than forcing the conclusion of a battle, and whoever does so first is sure to lose. This is the part of a fight that most captivates the audience, and in a boxing match, it begins more or less after the sixth round.

No doubt about it: Mingo and Oviedo are identical in skill, training and dexterity. In this regard, we're faced with an unproductive equilibrium, a perfect canceling out of strengths from which neither could emerge victorious. The fight, therefore, moves of necessity into the mental plane. It is here that all the variables independent of physical prowess begin to carry weight and to swing the balance in favor of one of the two rivals.

Mingo is desperate. He can't understand how a single man, a single small, old man, has managed to dispatch all of his boys. He can't understand how it is that he's spent half an hour sweating his ass off and he still hasn't managed to kill him. His mind grows distracted as he contemplates these uncertainties.

Oviedo is crazy and he doesn't think about anything.

Lunging at one another, Oviedo and Mingo end up in a bloody embrace. Their faces touch. The madman's, expressionless. The thug's, smiling.

Slowly, they pull apart. Oviedo is the first to relax his embrace and he releases Mingo, who begins vomiting blood. And not for nothing, given that Oviedo's Collins knife has punctured his abdomen.

Mingo falls dead, run through like a yaniqueque.

No one cheers.

Oviedo looks at his belly, in which Mingo's lengua de mime is buried up to the hilt.

He drops his Collins knife and, expressionless, as if he felt nothing, as if nothing hurt and nothing at all were really happening, he pulls out the lengua de mime with a precise yank. His vision begins to go dark. He falls to his knees and then falls face-first to the ground. All the women climb out of the pickup and surround Oviedo. They turn him over to see if he's still alive and realize that he's in the final throes. They stroke his face, they hug him, they comfort him, tropical Valkyries receiving—or sending off—the valiant warrior. Oviedo dies in their arms, a hint of a smile sketched on his face.

And while Inma was punishing Raúl and Oviedo was dying, Maceta was crossing the golf course, on his way back to Loco Abril's hut.

It's getting late.

Maceta pauses. He tilts his head. What he is witnessing is impossible.

Before him is a rainbow ending right in a sand trap . . . But the sprinklers are not on.

The sky is clear.

Maceta walks toward the sand trap and stops just where the rainbow ends.

He kneels. He has no shovel, only his hands.

He starts digging.

1965/1976

Inma was no virgin, we'll start with that, and Melisa and Clarisa knew when to wait outside the shack until their sister told them they could come in, even when it seemed like she was being hurt and especially if it seemed like she was being killed. But Inma had never taken so long to allow them inside before.

Melisa and Clarisa have run out of ways to entertain themselves: they've played jacks, they've played hopscotch, they've played marbles, they've played red light, green light, they've told riddles, they've told jokes, they've played charades . . .

They don't dare knock on the door.

They'd never be crazy enough to knock on the door.

Inside, Inma and Puro have spent the day naked, making love whenever the mood strikes them, and every time they try to get dressed they're defeated by an invincible lethargy. And so, they laze about on a threadbare mattress on the floor, playing, touching each other, pinching, laughing, caressing orifices, protuberances, bulges, plateaus, hills, towers, valleys, coves, deltas, bays, peninsulas, islands, plains and all other geographies with easy-to-parse double meanings, since the two of you are not idiots.

But afternoon falls and the saddest moment has arrived. Neither one wants to say goodbye, but say goodbye they must, so they start to get dressed.

Dressed at last, they stand facing one another: Puro, suitcase in hand, ready to go; Inma, with her face resting against his chest, ready to let him go. Goodbyes between lovers are bittersweet like this, because they combine the bitterness of parting with the sweetness of future reunion.

Molina, hiding behind a zinc wall, watches Inma's house. Horton comes up behind him.

"Nothing?"

Molina shakes his head and asks:

"What happened with Oviedo?"

"That crazy lady from intelligence went to soften him up a few hours ago . . . So we'll see."

Horton looks around, spellbound by the wretchedness of the shacks that are practically embedded in the immense garbage dump.

"You know what this place needs?" he asks Molina.

"What?"

"A flamethrower."

Molina laughs.

"I'd be more than happy to operate it myself," he says.

"I'm sure."

"I hate this place," Molina confesses. "I hate these people. All they do is complain and suffer and eat and beg . . . and fuck and have babies."

Horton smiles, but Molina is dead serious.

"So if you ever come across a flamethrower . . . give me a call."

"Maybe a bulldozer and a steamroller . . ." Horton murmurs to himself, fondling a private idea. "Get rid of all these shacks with a bulldozer; a grader to clear it . . . There was a place like this in Mackinaw. It got filled to the brim, of course . . . With garbage, not with people; we Americans have more dignity, not like here. A dump always fills up and the time comes when it can't take any more, and no one knows what to do. A guy came and bought it from the state. For peanuts, obviously! Well, it was a relief for the state to be rid of that blight on its landscape."

Molina looks at Horton, not understanding what he's talking about.

"And what that guy did was bring in a bunch of bulldozers and he covered the whole thing with gravel, and he covered the gravel with dirt. When he was finished, it looked like any old mountain, right? Well, every goddamned winter that mountain gets covered in snow and it turns into a ski hill. What do you think of that?"

Horton laughs.

"That's what you call using your noggin. That guy became a millionaire."

Horton falls silent and Molina watches him.

"Though, obviously, there's no winter here," Horton says, thinking aloud again. "It doesn't snow, I mean."

Molina opens his eyes wide, dubious.

"But I'm sure you could apply the same principle," mumbles Horton, lost in his daydream, "and put it to use for some . . . more spring-like sport."

Molina shakes Horton by the arm until he comes out of his reverie.

"The rabbit's out of the cave."

Indeed. Horton looks in the direction of Inma's shack and sees Puro come out, look around and walk away.

"I knew it," declares Molina, triumphant, unholstering his pistol. Horton does the same. The pair of them head toward their quarry.

Puro walks cautiously through the alleyways and corridors of the slum.

A whistle, like you'd use to call a dog.

Puro turns around and sees Molina and Horton aiming their weapons at him.

"Stop right there!" Molina shouts.

Puro starts running. He navigates the alleyways with Molina and Horton in hot pursuit. A breakneck race through that convoluted labyrinth of squalor.

Puro runs for his life, pushing people out of the way and leaping over obstacles. Horton and Molina do the same. Puro comes to a dead end. He scrambles to the roof of a shack and leaps into the garbage dump.

People who don't know their ass from their elbow associate garbage with rats. Others, who know even less, associate it with cockroaches. But in the tropics, garbage is not synonymous with rats or roaches, but rather with herons.

Herons love a landfill, a shithole, a dunghill. They're so lovely in flight, and even up close, with that pristine white plumage, and that chick-yellow-colored crest, and those long necks, folded back on themselves when they walk, elongated and straight when they fly. Don't even talk to this winged beast about seeking its sustenance in a lagoon, or in a pond, or in the mangrove, or on the backs of cattle swarming with ticks. For herons, nothing compares to a good garbage dump.

When Puro lands in the garbage dump, an immense flock of herons startles and takes flight. There are so many of them that everything Puro does from that moment on will occur beneath the shadow they cast as they fly from one end of the garbage dump to the other.

Puro is a tiny dot in that immense sea of garbage, darkened by a cumulonimbus of herons.

Horton and Molina are hot on his heels.

Puro runs between mountains of refuse.

He climbs, falls, gets back up, slips, tumbles, slides, but keeps running.

Horton and Molina come to a clearing. They appear to have lost him.

"There!" Molina points at Puro climbing up to a plateau of trash.

"Wait!" Horton suggests. "Let's split up."

Horton and Molina take off in different directions, circling the spot where they'd seen Puro, trying to trap him by pinching him off.

Molina and Horton advance through the garbage.

Puro, meanwhile, leans against an old bicycle in order to peek out over a hill of cardboard. The bicycle chain comes loose and falls to the ground, where it will remain until, a decade later, Maceta will unearth it and bestow it upon Chago.

Horton fires and misses. Puro ducks and advances in a crouch. As he does so, he kicks a Magic 8 Ball that rolls along until it comes to rest in the place from which it will not budge until it is discovered, years later, by Maceta, when it will come to mediate the constant misunderstandings between a father and his son.

Puro runs like a madman, going deeper and deeper into the landfill, where the heaps of rubbish are thicker and more irregular, making it impossible for him to run without tripping or getting tangled up or sinking.

He steps into a basketball hoop and falls. He gets up, runs, and a little farther on, kicks a bird feeder, injuring his big toe. Limping, he keeps going, and slips on a pile of vinyl records. He sits up and starts to crawl forward, when he is startled by his own reflection in the metallic surface of a strange mirror lodged among torn upholstery and rotten crates.

And so on.

Puro keeps running, sees Horton coming toward him and turns around. He hears a gunshot. Puro is still in one piece, but he sees Molina coming toward him from the other side. He's trapped.

Puro looks around, sees an old cookstove, runs toward it and opens it. He puts the suitcase inside the oven and keeps running, gaining enough ground to throw his pursuers off track, though they will certainly catch him. It's only a matter of time.

Indeed.

Puro rounds a garbage mound and comes face-to-face with Molina, who is pointing the pistol at him. He turns around and there is Horton. They've got him.

Puro pants, exhausted. Ditto for Horton and Molina.

"Where is it?" asks Molina, out of breath.

"Where is what?" says Puro.

A shot, and Puro folds in half, overcome with pain. He falls to his knees, then collapses face-first. Horton's pistol, trained on Puro, is still smoking. Molina is stunned.

Horton moves closer to make sure that Puro is dead. He nudges him with one foot.

"Why the hell did you do that?" asks Molina, livid.

"Well . . ."

"What do you mean, 'well'?"

"Mission accomplished."

"Mission accomplished?" Molina repeats, and then again, shouting: "Mission accomplished?"

"My mission at least," says Horton, defiant. "And yours too, I think, if I'm not mistaken."

Molina is apoplectic.

"And now how are we going to find the money?"

"Calm down."

"Calm down? You son of a bitch! Calm down?"

"Calm down. There was nothing in that bag," Horton explains. Now Molina looks confused.

"What?"

"At least nothing of value."

Molina looks at Horton, uncomprehending. Horton speaks to Molina with a certain air of superiority. Molina can't help feeling like an imbecile.

"There was no money . . . or gold. It was all a sham, a trick . . . to bring the moles out into the open."

Horton starts walking. His work is done. Molina, however, can't stop staring at Puro. He is horrified. Horton stops behind Molina, waiting for him.

"Come on. Let's go."

Molina's face turns hard.

"I thought we were going to let him live. You promised me. How am I going to explain this to my mother, Horton? What am I supposed to say to Mami now?"

A chick from every rooster.

"What do I know? The truth, maybe . . . ?"

"The . . . the truth." Molina rolls this around.

"Right."

"And . . . what is the truth?"

Horton grows impatient.

"That he died in battle . . . This is a war, remember? He's not the first and he won't be the last. Other mothers have also cried for their sons, on both sides, why would your mother be an exception?"

Molina comes up close to Horton.

"You lied to me! I was counting on that money! You made me believe there was money! I've done so much for you guys! If I had known that . . ."

Horton puts an arm around his shoulder as they walk.

"Easy, easy. Believe me, you'll be amply compensated by Uncle Sam for your extraordinary services."

Horton is leaning against his golf cart, smoking a cigarette. Another golf cart approaches in the distance. Horton drops the butt of the cigarette to the ground and steps on it. The approaching golf cart stops near the flag marking the ninth hole.

Molina climbs out and shakes hands with Horton. With a nod of his head and a smile on his lips, he shows the captain what he's just brought for him.

"Just as we agreed . . ."

They walk together toward the golf cart, inside which Lucía is seated, wearing a very pretty dress. The girl looks at the men, her brow furrowed. Horton looks at her with old hunger and pats his friend on the back.

"You've outdone yourself, my friend."

They laugh maliciously.

"I want to go home," Lucía says, not looking at them.

"I'll take you home myself, sweetie pie . . . in a little while."

Horton and Molina walk together toward the hole. Horton prepares his putt.

"We're square then?" Molina asks.

"Sí, señor. Yes, indeed."

"So, I can expect . . ."

"You can expect my unconditional financial backing and a broad and unquestionable triumph in the next elections; payment for a loyal servant."

They chuckle and shake hands.

In the distance, behind Molina, something catches Horton's eye. He runs back to his golf cart and grabs his binoculars.

"Oh, hell . . ." he says.

Far away from the men, Maceta is kneeling in a sand trap, digging.

Maceta removes the last fistfuls of dirt and considers what he's just found: the oven door from an old cookstove.

Maceta doesn't know what to do. He looks around. He turns back to the hole, reaches in, pulls on the handle, but the door is stuck. He pulls with all his might, but the door doesn't budge. He's halfway inside the hole, pulling with all his strength . . . The oven finally opens.

There is something inside. Maceta reaches in and pulls it out.

Puro's old suitcase is extremely heavy.

At just that moment, the barrel of a pistol comes to rest against Maceta's head.

"Well, well, well," says Horton, "look what we have here. I found our giant mole."

The significance of a pistol against his head is lost on the innocent Maceta, so he turns around as if nothing were out of the ordinary to look Horton over.

"A slum cockroach. Just as I suspected."

"Maceta!" Lucía shouts, running toward Maceta. Horton intercepts her.

"Maceta?" says Horton, trying to understand. "Maceta?"

Molina walks slowly toward the boy. Horton finally gets it and he starts to laugh. He studies the boy, not lowering the pistol from his face.

"But of course. He even has the same face," he says, then turns to Molina. "It would appear that your brother was taking care of the neighborhood sluts before I took care of him, eh?"

Molina walks up to Maceta. He yanks the suitcase out of his hands and walks a short distance away. He opens it and looks inside.

"What is that? What's in there?" asks Horton.

"What do you think it is, you supreme son of a bitch?"

Molina looks inside the suitcase again, just to be sure. Horton thinks about it.

"Naahh! It can't be. How?" he says.

"You told me there was nothing in here."

"Whoa! Wait just a minute! I never said there was nothing in there. I just said there was nothing of value."

"Oh, really? Does this look like nothing of value?"

Molina shows Horton the open suitcase. Horton takes a look and is startled. Molina starts to back up.

"What the fuck is that?"

Horton and Molina look at each other for a few tense moments. Lucía is still standing behind Horton. Maceta is still kneeling next to the hole. Molina closes the bag, walks over to Horton, takes Lucía by the hand and walks away.

"What are you doing?"

Molina ignores him.

"Molina!"

Horton fingers his pistol. Molina stops.

"Bring that girl back here, please," orders Horton. "And thank you very much for your services. You are dismissed."

"My services . . ." Molina repeats. "My services. It's not the first time I've heard you say that."

Molina still has his back turned. Horton does not see it when he takes the pistol from the waistband of his pants.

"Molina . . ."

"You know something, Horton?" says Molina, smiling. "Tomorrow, no one is going to miss us."

Molina turns around like a bolt of lightning and fires. Horton, by reflex, fires too. Lucía screams. Maceta runs to her and covers her with his body. Horton fires again. The bullet catches Maceta in the head and he collapses on top of Lucía, who is still screaming.

Molina keeps shooting and hits Horton in the stomach. Horton hits Molina in the chest. Wounded, they keep shooting until both of their pistols are empty.

They both fall to the ground. Horton is half-dead; Molina completely dead.

A few seconds later, Lucía crawls out from beneath Maceta. She turns his face and sees his bloody head. She cradles him. Cries.

"Maceta . . . Maceta . . ." Lucía says over and over through tears. The sun sets. Lucía cries harder.

"I'm sorry . . ." she sobs. "I'm sorry. Don't die. Don't die. I love you so much . . ."

But ay! Maceta kept dying.

Lucía cried what she needed to cry and not one tear more. She stands up and takes off running like a bat out of hell in search of help.

Soon the entire neighborhood is on the golf course. Picture it: everyone who lives on the street where Maceta lived, his greatest beneficiaries in front, in a procession headed by the very wild-looking Inma and the very hysterical Melisa and Clarisa.

Inma and her sisters throw themselves to the ground. Everyone else surrounds them. It's like what water buffalo do to protect their young from attacks by lions and leopards. Except here, the prey has already been taken down. No one seems to notice the other two bodies.

Molina was right.

Inma picks up her boy and leads the return procession.

The nearest hospital is for rich people. Well, let's just say it's not a hospital for poor people. But there's no other choice; the convoy heads in that direction.

The emergency staff snaps into action, but no doctor seems prepared to plunge into that pool of poverty stinking of wet cardboard, millipedes and moths.

"A doctor's on his way, he'll be here soon," a nurse insists. But no doctor comes and Maceta is dying.

And no one knows if the doctors have really been informed that there is a boy with a bullet wound to the face and they are declining the kind invitation, or if the emergency staff themselves, assuming majordomo duties, haven't even bothered to notify their superiors.

What is known is that Inma, the twins and the retinue are stirring up a lively ruckus. Someone offers to start a fistfight; someone ups the ante and recommends they set fire to the place. Yet another laments the dismal destiny that has tainted the Maceta bloodline, of which Ángel is the last bastion.

In an interior hallway, a doctor coming out of an exam room at just that moment pricks up her ears when she hears that surname, one you don't hear every day like you do Rodríguez, Pérez, González, Fernández or Martínez; one that belongs to the small cabal of names like Brazobán, Espíritusanto, Palofuerte, Roca, because the Cimarrones, no longer forced to adopt their tormentors' names, baptized themselves.

Her surname has that same flavor. Doctor Esmeralda Ruiz Palenque, who studied and earned her academic degrees at the University of Stalingrad through an athletic scholarship, clears a path through the staff milling about at the emergency room entrance. She's gained weight. Her days as a ping-pong champion are long gone, but the only thing she's lost is her figure, not her memory, and she bursts into the emergency room like a landslide.

With Maceta admitted and stabilized, the majority of the retinue returns to the neighborhood. Inma and her sisters remain.

Mercedes takes Amparo home. Lucía fights to stay as well, but she loses. She has not left her friend's side for one second. She does what she can and talks to Maceta without stopping, comforting him.

She can't go back to her own house; not right now.

Another tragedy awaits her there: Evelio realized—too late and, really, isn't this the tragedy of all gutless cowards?—that he'd had the nerve to sell his daughter, but that when it came to confronting his wife when she got home from work, he lacked two or three bushels of balls.

So, he shot himself through the roof of his mouth.

After they'd gathered Maceta up from the golf course, Lucía took charge of collecting his backpack, abandoned on the fallen tree trunk where he always left it before jumping the fence. She put it on her back and there was no force, human or divine, that could have taken it from her. She was the guardian of Maceta's possessions, end of story.

When they undressed Maceta and put him on the gurney to take him into the operating room, Lucía also took charge of his school uniform—which she folded carefully and placed inside the backpack—and the strange key he'd had hanging around his neck. When the members of the cortege that brought Maceta to the hospital began returning home, Lucía bid them farewell like a grown-up, expressing her appreciation for their solidarity, support and well-wishes. As if Maceta were her husband and she was dispatching visitors.

Unctuous children who are too big for their britches, the sort who chime in during adult conversations, or invite themselves along on adult outings, are well acquainted with these two expressions: "Children should be seen and not heard," and "You're going with the group that's staying." No one needed to say the first to Lucía, but they had to modify the second to make things crystal clear for her.

"You're staying, yes, with the group that's leaving," Eneida tells her. "Get your things."

They sleep that night at Inma's house: Eneida on Inma's pallet and Lucía in Maceta's padded drawer.

The sound of a rosary recited in the distance.

At the grocery store, inside which many worried neighbors are keeping vigil, Tomás and Simón ask the eight ball if Maceta will live.

The eight ball has given the same answer five times in a row: *Outlook not so good.*

Lucía gets up early the next day and starts doing chores before Eneida even wakes up. She tidies the little house, fetches water from the communal tap, lights the stove. Eneida gets up and helps her. Soon, Chago, Jacinto, Olivero and Don Jorge Aníbal arrive with coffee, bread, eggs, salami and taro. The adults have breakfast, but Lucía isn't hungry and she retreats to Maceta's box bed.

She opens the backpack and begins to read the notebook in which her friend records the natural history of a private world, complete with observed and described taxonomies, mechanisms explained, purposes intuited and even discovered. In the stilted, faux-scientific language of the entries, Lucía can recognize, more or less, the actual object that inspired them.

The actual object, Lucía thinks.

Who knows if the actual object is what Maceta says it is and it is she who is lost in a fantasy, in a delusion; she the one who is dreaming? A flat dream that is the result of the average of all interesting extremes; a mixture of gases that have individual and unique personalities, colors, reactivity and scent, but which, diluted into proportional parts of the surrounding air, become inert, noble, dead. A mediocre, average, middling, ordinary, run-of-the-mill, common dream in which things are what they are and behave accordingly. A dream devoid of magic, of fantasy; a dream in which all rules are obeyed because there is no other available path.

Mini Personal Jacuzzi, reads one of the entries, and Lucía knows that Maceta is referring to the rusted-out washbasin in which they used to bathe him when he was younger. *Kettledrum of Contemplation* is none other than the upside-down Mílex milk tin he sits on in the morning while he eats breakfast and thinks up the crazy thoughts that come to him as he watches his neighbors start their days. *Alien Laser Gun* is surely his name for the raised jack she'd so often seen him playing with, grasping, like a weapon, the lever that controls the platform when it lifts a vehicle.

Lucía takes Maceta's school uniform out of the backpack and, as she's about to put it away, she notices that there's something in the pants pocket. Lucía puts her hand in the pocket and extracts a very strange object, part artificial, part natural; part mechanical, part simple; part elemental, part composite.

What is this treasure?

Lucía consults the most recent dates in the catalog and does not find a name or a description that fits.

It's cylindrical in shape. Half of it is white, the other half metallic. A steel terminal sticks out of the white half, which is made of ceramic, and an almost fully intact ring juts out of the metallic half. In the center is a hexagonal nut.

None of the parts move.

Lucía stands up and goes over to face the adults. She announces that she's going out for some fresh air. Eneida says sure, but don't go too far. Lucía crosses the street and enters Lidio López Gutiérrez's Auto Body and Paint Shop. Several guys are in there working and they look at her with curiosity and surprise. Lidio is also working away, applying a thick coat of paint to a car with his left hand; his right, amputated at the elbow, is of little use to him. Or, of great use, especially when he uses it as an example, as a cautionary tale, or as a membership card to an exclusive and very small brotherhood of brave men.

"Cucuso," one of his employees calls out affectionately, and Lidio, as if coming out of a trance, raises his head. Lucía shows him the spark plug, held vertically between the tips of her thumb and forefinger.

"Greetings, Don Lidio," the girl says politely. "Please, what is this and what is it for?"

Lucía writes in Maceta's notebook.

PORTABLE SPARK. *Element that ignites a motor, so that it moves, a feeling, so that it is felt, an idea, so that*

it multiplies. Most prized possession of Ángel Maceta,
carried always in his pants pocket. Important that it
never be allowed to fall into the wrong hands.

Maceta hovered at the edge of death for three days. And when he woke up, the first word he said was my name.

"Lucía . . . Lucía . . . Lucía."

Clarisa, Melisa, Inma, Maceta and Amparo, the baby, left the neighborhood on a Palm Sunday, just after mass. They tied all their baskets and bundles into a pickup truck and hit the road. Actually, they only took some of their baskets and bundles; they gave most of their possessions to those who needed them more than they did.

They weren't the only ones to leave. We left too; Mami closed down the business and we moved a week after Maceta was discharged. Mercedes left, as I've already mentioned, and so did Jacinto and Eneida and their whole family.

But poverty is a revolving door. Not a day would pass before Inma's old shack would be occupied again, this time by an even larger family . . . And they'd be cooking again in the woodstove under the shade of the tamarind tree, and the laundry hanging on the clotheslines would return and return and return and return. And when those leave, others will come, and others and others and others . . .

For how long?

No one knows.

Near Inma's old shack there is a small, fenced-off shrine, inside of which are several candles, flowers, a figurine of the Virgen de la Altagracia, a set of commander's epaulets, and a photograph. The new residents of the neighborhood do not know the name of the young soldier in the photo, who cleansed his sins with blood and gave the only thing left to him, his own life's breath, so as to cast a small light on the bounded darkness of misery.

And every year, more or less on the same date, a group of elegant, well-dressed, middle-aged women arrive in nice cars, accompanied by well-fed sons and daughters, and they change the candles, swap out the flowers, clean, paint if painting is needed, talk amongst themselves, and finally they pray, observe a moment of silence, say goodbye to one another and depart.

Their sons and daughters watch them work, amazed by the persistent ritual, which they have no idea why they have to attend . . . not knowing that their mothers are doing them a great favor, that they are sharing with their children a gift of incalculable value.

Because poverty has no memory.

It thrives in the wasteland of forgetting. It spreads like wildfire.

Only those who remember can vanquish it and . . .

"Oh, Mom, for the love of God, don't ruin it," says Doris.

"You were doing so well," Iris stresses. "But you went a little overboard with the proletarian rhetoric."

2017

Raising twin girls is no cakewalk. Especially when you get a pair like these two.

Twins don't run in my family, not identical or any other kind. It's a legacy of the Carmona family and Ángel must have passed it along to me like a penalty, like a war tax, a toll.

He says that identical twins are a lottery and that it's not genetic.

Yeah, right . . .

The truth is you should think carefully before having certain men's children.

I adore them, but coño . . . My fear was that they'd come out taciturn like their father, but it was even worse than that: they came out just like me.

And two of them.

They never shut up, they're impatient, they stick their noses into everything, and they're always showing off. It was a miracle that I was able to finish telling them the story, and they're not even letting me finish telling it properly.

"So," says Doris, the one who loves the shoot-'em-up parts, "this Mexican soap opera of yours has like two hundred holes in it."

"Holes?" I exclaim, and my mind goes straight to the holes Ángel used to make in Horton's golf course. Physically, they are the spitting image of their maternal grandmother. People say they got their elbows and the knuckles on their toes from me, but those eyes they're looking at me with are mine, and that hair, and that annoying little voice . . .

God bless them.

"And," says Iris, the romantic one, "you said you were going to tell us absolutely everything."

Get a load of this girl. I've always felt a certain I don't know what about scolding them or giving them a good thrashing, because it feels like I have two Inmas sitting in front of me. Certain insolence I just have to let slide.

"I did tell you everything," I say, containing myself.

"A bloodbath," Iris replies.

"I warned you about that right from the beginning."

"That's not the problem," Doris clarifies.

"What is the blessed problem, then?"

"You said they shot Daddy in the head," Iris protests, "but that's clearly impossible."

"Horton shot *at* his head," I explain. "But the bullet only grazed him. He lost a lot of blood."

"Then why didn't you tell it like that right at the start?"

See what I mean?

"I didn't tell it like that because, at that moment, when it happened, I thought they'd blown his brains out. I was a child, if you'll recall."

"But now you're an adult," responds Doris, who never loses a fight, "and you're telling us the story now, not when you were a kid. You knew they hadn't shot him in the head."

I sigh.

"They fired at his head, period," I say, fuming. "Obviously, the bullet only grazed him. Next hole."

They exchange looks, contrite. Sometimes I have to raise my voice with them. Iris takes the helm.

"What happened with Captain Horton? And with his wife?"

"Mrs. Horton divorced the captain within a year and moved to Santiago with some big shot involved with the government. Now that he was single, the captain brought a new little number home with him every three months or so, but he was played out. He had cancer. He closed the golf course and left. He was hospitalized in Baltimore. He lasted two years and then the devil took him. They buried him up there somewhere."

"Who cares about Horton?" Doris argues. "Finish telling us what happened with the treasure! Obviously, they went looking for it."

"Obviously. Where do you think the money for your aunts' salon came from? And the school remodel? And the construction of the Juan Oviedo Sports Complex? And the upkeep of the Puro Maceta Health Center? And the funding for the Francisco Carmona Bank for Small and Medium-Sized Enterprises? And to pave all those streets? And to pay Amparito's school fees? And to send your father abroad to study? And me too? And all the other kids who . . ."

"Okay, okay, okay, we understand!" they shout in unison.

"Your grandmother still had a lot of contacts in the black mar . . . in the streets. Don Pancho's old associates. It was no problem to liquidate the ingots. They didn't get all of the money, of course. Every crook involved in the deal took his cut. Even so, Inma ended up with most of it. We never lacked for anything ever again. Not for things we needed, or for things we wanted."

Inma had her share of boyfriends too, always younger than her and always temporary, never quite up to the task. "My little pets," she called them, "to warm my bed when needed." Tígueres, I called them, kept men, freeloaders. "Don't think that I wouldn't have had to support Puro too," she said to me one time after hearing me describe her boyfriend du jour. "That one lived with his head in the clouds."

I know all about that.

Now she's with a more serious man, her age, a cardiologist, a widower, rolling in dough. He's with Inma because he loves her, not because he needs her, and isn't that, after all, the difference between being poor and being rich? We've all got our fingers crossed that this one will last and there are even rumors of an engagement.

Clarisa and Melisa both married good men, professionals, men who like to come home after work and spend time with their kids, three apiece. And they know all about the twins' past, because it was the first thing they told those men when they first fell in

love, so they wouldn't suddenly change their tune and start acting like jackasses when they found out about it later.

Aside from the ingots, Inma and the twins gathered up all of
Oviedo's belongings, sorted and organized them and put them
into storage. To my understanding, that is the real treasure:
hundreds of photographs, documents, telegrams, letters and
newspaper clippings that paint a very different picture of the
Dominican Civil War and to which no historian has ever had
access . . . Except me. I used them for my doctoral thesis. I've
got both Princeton and Johns Hopkins champing at the bit for
the manuscript.

"And what about Don Chago?" asks Iris.

"Buried in the Villa Mella Cemetery. He spent his last years
on the ranch that Inma bought for him in Hato Mayor. He became
quite the gentleman farmer. They visited him regularly. He died
of diabetes. He wouldn't let them take him to a hospital. He invited
his friends, Inma, your father, a few sisters he had in El Seibo. He
left instructions that he be taken to where his mother was buried. He bid farewell to everyone and he died."

"Tomás and Simón?" inquires Doris.

"Tomás was killed in a holdup. Simón emigrated to New York
and married a gringa over there. He opened a store and is doing
really well."

I don't tell them this, but Simón still has the eight ball, only
now he begins his questions by saying "Papá," because he swears
that Tomás is advising him from the hereafter through the ball.

My daughters look at one another and then look at me. I know
what they want to ask, but they won't do it. Iris lowers her eyes,

but Doris's expression turns hard. If one of them is going to ask, it'll be Doris. But she doesn't do it. I'll have to help them.

"Your grandfather, Evelio, did not die of a heart attack," I tell them without preamble. Iris raises her eyes again and Doris's expression softens.

"It happened just like I told you. Now you'll understand why your Grandma Tudi doesn't have a single photo of him in her house. And why she refuses to go with us to the cemetery when we go to visit his grave . . ."

I know what Doris is thinking. I can read it in her face.

"It's not your grudge," I tell her, "so let it go. I've got all I can take with Mami and her resentment, and Lord knows I've tried to reason with her. It was a long time ago, and if you remember the worst about a person rather than the best of them, all it does is rot your soul. We must let the dead rest in peace, otherwise they move into your head and stink up your life."

Doris nods.

"Learn from your father's example," I conclude. "He's been my best teacher."

They burst out laughing.

Phew!

That was intense. But I think we've now fielded that ball once and for all. Although you never know. We'll see what happens the next time I announce that it's our day to visit the cemetery.

They're in a good mood. They're hungry, but they haven't said anything. They don't need to: I can hear their stomachs growling. And it didn't start just now, no. It's been a while, but they didn't want to ask for dinner and interrupt the story.

I hear the door. I hear my husband's footsteps as he comes home from work and, as always, I have the urge to leave these two midsentence and run to him and seize him and hug him in my arms and beg him to take me far away, to the ends of the earth, just the two of us, to take me all over again to all the countries we've visited, or to take me to the countries we have yet to see, and to tell me the story of what he sees, to explain to me the meaning of the temples and paintings and statues and rock formations and animals in those regions, to tell me the story of the constellations that adorn the night skies in those places.

But . . .

"Well, there's just one more thing then . . ." Iris announces.

"What?"

"What do you mean 'what'?" says Doris, indignant. "You know perfectly well what!"

"What was in the suitcase?" they say together.

I start to laugh.

"A good question, indeed," says Ángel, peeking into the room from the threshold.

Life is long and within it one meets a multitude of people, each one of them different. How is it possible that I fell in love with this man? Easy. With him I become that little girl waiting on the bench at school for him to bring offerings of incalculable and mysterious treasures.

What are you gonna do?

That and also, over time, Maceta turned into a big, tall moreno with a penetrating gaze and an enigmatic temperament, an easy conversationalist who melted the heart of any woman he met.

Or maybe he just melts mine.

I don't know. What I can say for sure is that I always found him handsome and I still find him handsome, now more than ever, because that scar that marks the corner of his right eye, like the tail of a comet, is the secret ingredient that changed Maceta into Ángel, the boy into the man.

Ángel enters the room. He's holding the famous suitcase and he places it before them.

"Come on, see for yourselves."

The girls both lunge for the bag.

"Give it to me!" Doris screams, snatching the case from her sister.

"Idiot!" Iris screams, taking it back.

"Me first!" Doris insists.

"You second!" Iris mocks, because really, she only pretends to be the goody-two-shoes and the only actual difference between the two girls is that one asks for water and the other says "I'm thirsty."

I knew this would be a bad idea. Sometimes I can't believe they're almost sixteen years old.

Luckily, the suitcase, being such an important souvenir for Ángel and for me, is always well stocked with the thing it guards best.

Ángel takes it from them. He opens it.

"Peace, peace!" he says, handing them out.

EPILOGUE

Those know-it-all girls never asked me about Sarah. And they should have asked me.

After what happened she left the island, no one knew for where. What I have been able to find out is that a court-martial awaited her in her native United States—or better yet, awaits her still, since there's no statute of limitations on her offense. The charge: high treason. I'm sure it didn't take them long to discover the three lumps of painted lead that she had placed in the ship's vault.

One day while I was studying at Leiden University, I received a postcard with a photo of the Potemkin Steps in Odessa, Ukraine. On the back, written in a leftward- slanting hand with lots of lovely little curlicues, it said: *Loved your paper.*

The brief message was unsigned.

My bones turned to ice and my heart nearly leapt out of my mouth. By some miracle, I didn't vomit up my heart, but I did lose my breakfast.

I had recently published an essay in *Foreign Affairs* about US intervention in the Dominican Republic in 1965.

And she'd loved it.

For three months I waited for the sniper bullet that would put an end to me, for the team of mercenaries that would kidnap me in the dead of night, for the knife that would slit my throat while I slept. I ate only what was strictly necessary in order not to starve to death, convinced that my meals were poisoned.

Inma came to visit me toward the end of that period. She was on her way back from Switzerland, where Ángel was completing a postdoctoral fellowship at the Large Hadron Collider (does it come as a surprise to anyone that Maceta became an experimental physicist?) and she stopped by to see me.

The second I saw her on my doorstep I threw myself into her arms, weeping.

I told her everything. When I finished, Inma pulled a postcard with a photo of the Kamianets-Podilskyi Castle out of her purse. There was no message on the back.

"Maceta got one of the Freedom Square in Kharkiv," she told me.

"What did it say?"

"The same as mine," replied Inma. "Zilch."

"And so?"

"You know how that boy is," said Inma. "He didn't think twice about it."

"She's in Ukraine."

"The last place that skank would be is in Ukraine. Don't be a fool."

"Where then?"

"Juan Dolio."

The tostones Inma had made me while we were talking turned in my stomach.

"What?"

"Relax. This is old news. What she wanted to tell us, she's already told us. And what she needed from us, she already has. There will be no more postcards."

So, she got her cut too. Inma tells me that she has a glass eye, that she's older and more wrinkled than the hide on an elephant's ass, and she spends her time at the beach putting the sanquis to work.

And I'll relax when they tell me she's dead.

The truth is, I don't know when any of us will be able to relax. Or at least me, since Ángel is oblivious and Inma isn't afraid of anyone or anything.

Just as an example:

Last summer, Yubelkis, who emigrated to Rhode Island, came to spend her vacation with Clarisa and Melisa. The three families rented a villa together in Casa de Campo. In the evening, the men went off separately to drink, like men always do, and Clarisa and Melisa and Yubelkis remained alone in the pool.

After about five beers, Yubelkis told the twins that when Oviedo was killed, she kept his two Collins knives and Mingo's lengua de mime.

She kept them for years.

"One night," Yubelkis confesses, "this was when I was still living here, in Evaristo, there's a knock at the door and I say to myself, it can't be Roberto because he's staying with his dad this weekend, and I hadn't made plans with anyone else at that hour. It was like eleven at night and it was pouring rain and I was bundled up from head to toe, watching a movie. They knock and knock. And I'm thinking, who could it be? And shit, because if it turned out to be a delivery guy with the wrong address and I had to get out of bed for him, there was gonna be trouble. I get up, throw on a bathrobe and go to the door. And there in the doorway is a Haitian wearing a red shirt and tight jeans and a bunch of bracelets and chains and a nice pair of shoes. Guy looks real smooth, and he's completely dry, as if it's not coming down in buckets out there. I stand there staring at him and he stands there staring at me. I don't close the door on him, I can't, I swear on my mother's soul, I can't, and I think, this pití put a hex on me and I didn't even realize it. Then he raises his eyebrows, like he's saying, 'Well, then?' And that's when it dawns on me who this dude is and what it is he wants. I go back to my bedroom, look under the bed and pull out Mingo's lengua de mime. I go back to the door with the lengua de mime in my hand, but the Haitian is gone. I think, he's in the house. I grip the lengua de mime and I start searching the house. Nothing. He's not there. My hand starts to hurt, I'm gripping the knife so hard. I look down at my hand and the lengua de mime is gone too. I open my hand and all that's inside is a tiny seashell."

ACKNOWLEDGMENTS

The story of Maceta is primarily the story of an invincible child. I conceived of the story and wrote it in 2014. The first to read it was Ernesto Alemany, who fell in love with it, and instantly recognized its cinematic potential. His enthusiasm was extremely important and also contagious, and his suggestions and comments, both intelligent and spot-on, helped me to define the narrative arcs of the main characters. My first words of thanks go to Ernesto. Without his involvement, neither this novel nor its film adaptation would exist.

This novel and its movie version would also not exist without Linel Hernández, who is a glass of water and a sunny day and a cool breeze; anyone who knows her knows that I'm not exaggerating. I owe the book's title to her and the film producers owe her for the acquisition of the story. Linel is a member of a very small group of people without whom nothing would ever happen in the world, a carbon atom who carries, brings, weaves and produces the molecules necessary for the creation of living organisms. Thank you, Li.

Thank you as well to Professor Rubén Silié, who one day, many years ago, entertained me with tales of the revolution. Of all his stories, none seemed as wonderful to me as his journey along the malecón, transporting, along with some other boys, a cache of rifles without firing pins. A writer is never certain when an anecdote as good and as purposeful as this one will emerge from the seas of memory. I am fortunate indeed to have friends like Professor Silié.

Doctor Luis Scheker Ortiz, kindred spirit and surrogate father, has given me many gifts in this lifetime, and among the most important are his lessons about Juan Bosch, whom he took me to meet one morning more than twenty years ago. I remember that, during the visit, I said not a single word, young, timid and awkward as I was, and Don Juan asked me if the cat had gotten my tongue. Oh, youth! Thank you, Don Luis, for taking part in mine.

During that same period, Don Luis took me to meet another important figure whom I would like to thank now, posthumously: Pedro Mir. I modeled Maceta in part on this profoundly human, exquisite, formidable, erudite, compassionate and curious man. We spoke on two different occasions. He had emphysema and would grow quickly tired, but it couldn't diminish the passion with which he spoke about two topics of fundamental importance to him at that time: the Dominican Civil War and the recent invention of the internet, to which, by his own admission, he was completely addicted.

The talented, cheerful and marvelous Nashla Bogaert fell in love with the story and particularly with Inma, my favorite character. I am grateful for the enormous sensitivity with which she understood and interpreted this fabulous, complex and contradictory woman, and for the affection with which, alongside Gilberto Morillo and David Maler, she nurtured the film adaptation of my *Reinbou*.

Voltaire's Candide, Professor Pangloss's star pupil, believed that we live in the best of all possible worlds. Others, like myself, respectfully differ. But this does not mean I can't admire those blessed with the startling capacity to understand the world in the best possible way, all evidence to the contrary. The universe, after all, is a phenomenon that occurs strictly inside our brains, so it should come as no surprise that these sorts of people are happy, come what may.

My son Thiago and my wife Wara belong to this cabal of grinners, and I am grateful every day for the lessons I learn simply by watching them live. That's why this book comes from the two of them and is for the two of them.

ABOUT THE AUTHOR

Pedro Cabiya is a Puerto Rican writer who has lived for the past two decades in the Dominican Republic. He is the author of 13 books and over 100 essays and articles. His work has been recognized by PEN Club International, the Institute of Puerto Rican Literature, and the Association of Dominican Writers and Journalists. In 2014 he was awarded the prestigious Caonabo de Oro for excellence in letters.

ABOUT THE TRANSLATOR

Jessica Powell has published translations by Pablo Neruda, Sergio Missana, Gabriela Wiener and Silvina Ocampo, among others. Her translation of *Wicked Weeds* (Mandel Vilar Press) by Pedro Cabiya was named a finalist for the 2017 Best Translated Book Award, made the longlist for the 2017 National Translation Award and was a 2016 Forward Indies Winner.